# When Love Stands in the Way

## Mary Denise

Published by Dolphin Star

Dolphin Star

ISBN: 978-1-7379124-2-2
Cover Design by Loren John Presley

First Edition

## *Dedication*

This is my first book and I would like to dedicate my book to my three gorgeous babies. Stevie Chartene, Samantha Rae, and Adams James.

Remember to always show respect, and you will be given respect. Show love, and you will be loved. Always stay strong for each other, and always tell the truth. No matter how it may hurt, we can always fix the truth. But a lie we can't fix because it's a lie. Always be there for each other, with respect.

Love you all,
Mommy

# My Next Love

I love the fact that we are friends first. I love the way we laugh together. I love the fact you are the person you are. I love the way you are with me. I love the way we sleep together, when I am in your arms.  I love the touch of your arms. I love the touch of your hands, the taste of your lips, and the smell of you.

I love the way I have to touch you all the time. Most of all, I love the way you look at me. When our eyes meet the love you have for me is just amazing. You wake me every morning with a smile on your face, and I love the fact that we are blessed every day!

I love the way you love me because your love is what means the most to us.

-Mary Denise

# Table of Contents

# Chapter 1

Anna had two children: a son and a daughter, whom she had with her husband Allan. When her son was eight and her daughter five, Anna took on a new job that required her to travel across various parts of the United States. Each week, she would fly from Redding, California to Las Vegas, Nevada.

For one week out of every month, Anna lived in Las Vegas with another man named Tom; it was during this time they conceived their daughter together. Carrying the child until she started showing, Anna then returned home and began telling Allan and her two children, Alex and Amanda, that she needed to travel to New York for approximately three months, or potentially longer.

While pregnant with her first baby from her second husband, Anna took the newborn, Alyssa, back to her family in Redding. She explained to them all that Alyssa was a friend's daughter—another coworker's—and that she had been watching her until the mother could return after having another child. Amanda asked about the baby's name, and Anna said it was

Alyssa.

When the second baby arrived from Tom, Anna once again left for New York, claiming this time to be gone for seven months. She returned home briefly and, when questioned about appearing more rounded, she quipped about all the "good sandwich places" in New York that had contributed to her growing belly.

She named her second daughter Amber. It was evident that Amber resembled Anna greatly, and thus, unlike Alyssa, Anna did not bring her back to Redding with her. Tom found it challenging to care for the infant on his own and insisted that if Anna couldn't be more present, she would have to give up her job.

Anna then adjusted her schedule to visit Redding only twice a month and once told Allan they would have to come and see her in New York. For three years following Amber's birth, Anna decided against having any additional children, leaving her with four kids—two from each relationship.

Allison was the third child born to Anna and Tom together. Born six weeks premature, but healthy. For Anna, Allison was the cherished 'apple' of her eyes.

When Anna returned to Redding with a three-month-old Allison in tow, Allan expressed an interest in visiting New York for the weekend so they could spend time together as a family. Anna agreed, planning to host them at her friend's house in New York, which had a designated baby room.

As the appointed weekend arrived, Anna navigated the delicate task of explaining Allison's existence to Allan and the children without revealing too much prematurely. Using her friend's place for their visit, Anna prepared for the difficult conversation ahead.

During that Friday in New York, when the door opened unexpectedly, Anna was overjoyed to see Alex and Amanda rushing into her arms.

"Whose baby is this?" Amanda asked curiously.

Anna, overwhelmed by exhaustion and emotional strain, directed Amanda to take Allison upstairs as she and Allan needed to talk. Allan soon entered the room, his expression one of confusion and hurt.

"How could you have another man's baby?" he inquired, his voice laced with defeat.

"Allan," Anna began, trying to explain, "Allison is our daughter. I didn't know about her until it was too late; I went into labor unexpectedly at work. She is ours now."

She urged him to see the tiny child for himself, hoping that would reassure him of their shared parenthood.

"Go get the baby," Allan commanded after a moment of silence.

Anna called Amanda down again with Allison, and as Allan held his daughter, he scrutinized her features, his doubt evident. "This is not my daughter," he stated flatly, turning to Anna. "Whose baby is this?"

In that moment of uncertainty and vulnerability, Anna could only affirm, "She is our daughter now."

Allan handed the baby back to Anna, then told Amanda to fetch her brother.

"We're leaving," Allan announced, his voice heavy with resolve.

That night, Anna faced immense fear and isolation with tiny Allison in her arms. She dialed Allan's number repeatedly, but he didn't answer; neither did Alex or Amanda. Even their home phone remained silent, denying her the comfort of connection.

***

Allan, Alex, and Amanda returned home in a heavy silence; tension hung thick between them.

"Who does the baby belong to, Dad?" Alex eventually broke the quiet.

Allan continued to stare out the aircraft window as it soared beyond the clouds.

"Your mother said she is ours," he replied, his voice calm but betraying an underlying strain.

"But the baby doesn't look like any of us at all," Alex observed. "Dad, is mom seeing another man?"

Allan's exterior remained stoic and unruffled, while inside he was struggling to maintain control over his emotions—a battle he fought with every breath.

"I don't know," he admitted, his words measured.

That night when they arrived home, Allan excused himself, telling his children he had something to attend to before retreating into his room. He then took the decisive step of hiring a private investigator to follow Anna and uncover the truth about her activities.

Anna anticipated this move and adjusted her behavior accordingly, staying in New York for an entire month without contacting Tom. The only update Allan received from the investigator was that Anna appeared to truly love Allison; she even brought the baby to work with her. Although this reassurance provided some comfort, Allan's gut feeling remained unsettled.

Two weeks after the private investigator's surveillance concluded, Anna dialed Allan again. This time, he answered.

"Allan, I'm so sorry I never told you about Allison," Anna confessed.

"Okay, Anna, come home. For good this time," Allan responded, his tone firm yet gentle.

"For good?"

"I don't want you going anywhere without me from now on," Allan explained. "We're a team, Anna, and I no longer feel secure about you traveling alone for work after what has happened. I have the right to be with you and know where you are."

Anna understood his perspective and, for the moment, agreed to the arrangement.

Allison had grown; she was now six months old and Anna often remarked, *"She's as cute as hell."* Upon landing, Anna took her time disembarking, careful with the baby in her arms. That's when she spotted Allan off in the corner of the airport, and her heart swelled with joy at the sight of him. As they embraced, Allan took charge of her luggage so Anna could hold their daughter.

For weeks following that reunion, Allan shunned any involvement with Allison's care. Amanda and Alex, however, were delighted to welcome their mother and new sister into their lives. They bonded quickly, with Amanda taking a particular liking to holding her sibling and Alex enjoying feeding her bottles and offering comforting holds.

One evening, Anna's phone rang; she answered, only to hear Tom, her other husband, on the line. Keeping her voice low, Anna continued the conversation as she stepped into the bathroom for privacy. Allan overheard snippets of their conversation.

"Yes, Honey, I've been fine... Sure, in fact, Allison and I will be home on Friday," Anna said into the phone, her words barely audible.

Allan's heart sank, feeling defeated by what he suspected to be true.

When Anna emerged from the bathroom, Allan blocked her exit, his eyes locking onto hers with an intense stare that stopped her in her tracks.

"You have forty-five minutes to get yourself and that fucking Tom's kid out of my house!" he bellowed, his voice laced with anger. "Don't you say one word to me, or my two children from that lying mouth of yours. I will be back after you are gone."

"Allan then shouted for Alex and Amanda, who hurriedly climbed into the car as it drove away." The kids bombarded him with questions throughout their journey.

Allan eventually halted the vehicle in front of a restaurant, instructing everyone to "be quiet and let's eat dinner."

Back at her phone, Anna called Tom back. "Tom, we're on the 7:00 p.m. plane. We'll meet you in Vegas an hour later," she said, her voice steady despite the turmoil.

Reunited with family, Alyssa and Amber were ecstatic to see their mother and baby sister Allison. Tom seemed equally delighted by the reunion.

Upon returning home without Anna or Allison, Allan gathered Alex and Amanda for an explanation. But as he started speaking, the phone rang once more.

"Is that mom?" Alex inquired.

"Don't answer," Allan instructed. "If she leaves a voicemail, I'll listen to it."

***

Two weeks after Allan sought Anna's address to send divorce papers, he called again but didn't get through. Meanwhile, Alex and Amanda had heard nothing from their mother, fostering a growing sense that the new baby held more significance than they did in their father's eyes.

Alex was nearing his 18th birthday, which loomed just three months away.

When Allan's call to Anna went unanswered, he spent an entire night holding her pictures, tears streaming down his face in solitude and desolation. Upon hearing his father's sorrowful cries and seeing him huddled with photographs of their mother, Alex quietly closed the bedroom door behind him—his young heart brimming with anger.

The following morning, Alex reached out to Anna privately, ensuring no one else could hear what he had to say. When her phone rang and she saw it was from Alex, she answered, only to be met with a torrent of his fury.

"How dare you bring another man's child into our home and try to pass her off as my father's kid? You are one sick bitch! And you just need to leave us three alone and sign my father's divorce papers so we can move on with our lives! Never call me again! Never talk to me again!" Alex bellowed, his words a stark rebuke.

Before he could hang up, Anna managed to interject, "I love you, my only son!"

Alex shared the conversation with Amanda later that day after picking her up from school. She looked at him with disbelief and said, "How can you say those things to mom? All because she wanted a baby and daddy didn't want any more kids, so mommy had one with somebody else! If you and dad don't see that she did bring the baby back to us, right Alex?"

Alex met his sister's gaze, feeling baffled by her understanding. Despite this, he had already expended much emotional energy for the day.

"Amanda, sometimes you just don't get it," Alex replied, his voice edged with frustration.

Back at home, they found their mother there with all three of her daughters from Tom. Upon seeing Anna, Amanda rushed into an embrace, while Alex walked right past her as if she were invisible.

8

Amanda was taken aback when Anna introduced her new sisters, Alyssa, Amber, and Allison. "Wow! I have three sisters now!" Amanda exclaimed in disbelief.

Not even ten minutes passed before Allan arrived with his car, filled with tension. As he stepped out, his voice was laced with anger. He instructed Amanda to go inside but she defiantly replied, "No! If you guys are fighting, I'll take my new sisters and go sit with them in Mommy's car."

Allan's shouts at Anna escalated until he locked eyes with her, his words cutting sharply through the air. "If I were you, I would get back into that car and drive away, never looking back at me or my two kids again!" His hand then swung in a swift, harsh slap to her face, commanding her departure with a clear instruction on how to send divorce papers.

Anna screamed back at him, declaring she'd have everything they owned through legal means and more. She walked away, leaving the scene behind.

Amanda refused to budge from Anna's car; together, they drove off with all four daughters in tow. Allan bombarded her phone with calls, voicemails insisting on the return of his daughter. Before reaching their new home, Anna called him back. "Mandy is my daughter too, Allan, and she'll stay here until she chooses to return," she asserted.

When they arrived at their temporary residence, Anna made it clear to Amanda: "You are my brother's child. You must call me Aunt Anna. Do you understand?" All Amanda could muster was a simple, "Yes, Aunt Anna."

Upon entering the house, Tom greeted Amanda with surprise and curiosity, asking why he hadn't been told about her sooner.

The dynamics in the household were shifting, but Amanda found the title of 'Aunt Anna' unsettling. Meanwhile, Tom went about his evening routine every night, until a troubling incident occurred.

One evening when Anna was away in New York for work, and Amanda was left to babysit, Tom beckoned her to his room under the guise of needing help. The situation quickly escalated; he threw her onto the bed and assaulted her.

The following night, Tom had a casual phone call with Anna, keeping the incident secret from her. After they exchanged goodbyes, Tom attacked Amanda again.

Desperate for help, she phoned her father while Tom was asleep early that morning and detailed everything that had happened under Tom's abuse. Allan, understanding the urgency, raced through the night, arriving at 3:30 a.m.

As Allan approached the house, he called out to Amanda on her phone; she gathered her belongings quickly, noting Tom was asleep and deeply intoxicated—the pattern of his crimes becoming all too clear. She fled to her father's arms and together they sped away to the Sheriff's office.

The sheriff arrived promptly at Allan's car, and Amanda recounted every harrowing detail, even admitting to being forced to call Anna 'Aunt Anna'. As a result of Amanda's testimony, Tom was arrested and taken into custody.

Meanwhile, the three younger girls were placed in state care pending their mother's return. Despite numerous attempts by Allan to reach her, Anna remained unreachable; he eventually left an urgent voicemail:

"Anna, it's me. I'm with Mandy now; she's safe. The other girls are in state care. Tom has been arrested – he raped our daughter. Please call me back."

Upon receiving the message and piecing together the gravity of the situation, Anna was consumed by a whirlwind of emotions.

She refused to believe Tom had harmed her children. She only felt betrayed by Allan—in her mind, this was a ploy at retaliation.

# Chapter 2

The weight of the day pressed down heavily on Anna as she disembarked from her plane. Her steps were quick as she made her way directly to the jailhouse where Tom was being held.

Approaching the reception area, she explained she wanted to see Tom face-to-face. The sheriff, who had been involved in Tom's arrest, met Anna outside of Tom's visitation room. His expression was one of sympathy and understanding.

"Are you going to bail him out?" the sheriff asked gently, his voice laced with concern.

Anna shook her head, unable to speak past the lump in her throat. The sheriff led her inside, where she confronted Tom through the glass partition.

Anna looked into Tom's eyes. He was still very drunk.

"Take him back," Anna said, her own thoughts a blur. "I don't want to see him."

The sheriff nodded and took Tom away without another

word. Once he had left, Anna's knees buckled; she crumpled to the floor, sobs shaking her body as she felt her life was split in two. If she hadn't taken Amanda back home with her, Allan wouldn't have had this opportunity to do this to her.

As she sobbed, she could overhear the Sheriff talking on the phone with his own wife—she was watching over the three daughters Anna had with Tom.

The following morning, Alyssa, Amber, and Allison would go home safe with their mother, but Amanda would go home with Allan. Little Amber and Alyssa hugged Anna tightly when they were reunited. Baby Alisson would be too young to remember anything that transpired last night.

As the girls finally succumbed to sleep the following evening after dinner, Anna sat alone in the quiet house, lost in thought. She reflected on the past six months and all that had led up to this moment – the realization that she needed to be strong not just for herself, but for her children.

Tom called later that night, finally sober, as he tried to apologize—though Anna interrupted him and apologized first for Allan trying to pull the stunt, and that she would bail him out soon.

Tom played along, but told Anna he had bailed himself out, and mentioned he was staying somewhere else. He had to, due to child protection services.

Legal proceedings moved swiftly between Anna and Allan following these events, and soon enough Allan was awarded custody of their two youngest children. Visitation rights were granted to Anna, but they came with stringent conditions and supervision by a caseworker.

The final blow came during Alex's 18th birthday celebration, an event Allan hosted without Anna's involvement. The pain of exclusion was acute, a harsh reminder of the new normal she had to accept.

***

Amidst the tumultuous sea of change, a momentous occasion awaited Allan and Alex at their home. Allan ushered Alex outside, guiding him to the driveway where an unfamiliar truck gleamed under the afternoon sun.

"Happy birthday, son," Allan said as he handed over the keys to the new vehicle. "This is for you, as long as you stay committed to your education."

Alex was stunned in front of his father. His eyes lit up at the sight of his own name plate on the truck and the promise it represented.

"Thanks, Dad," Alex managed to say, feeling the weight of responsibility now paired with opportunity. "I won't let you down."

The significance of this gift wasn't lost on Allan. It was more than just a vehicle; it was a symbol of hope and a new chapter for both father and son. He could see the determination in Alex's eyes, a reflection of his own ambitions years ago.

As they stood together, Allan added, "Make sure you call your mother. She should know about this."

Alex hesitated. "Dad," he spoke seriously. "I told Mom to

just fuck off."

"What?" Allan asked.

"I saw you crying, holding her pictures," Alex explained. "She hurt you so bad. She hurt us...so I called her and told her I'm never speaking to her again."

Allan took a short moment to think as the two stood in the driveway. "Think hard about that," he said stoically. "And I'm not talking to you as a father to a child on this, but man-to-man."

"You really think I will?" Alex asked. "You, even after everything she did to you?"

"I would like you to be careful about cutting her off entirely. Yes, what she did hurt us, but there's still humanity in her. One day, that humanity might show through and surprise you. If it does, I hope you won't have too many regrets."

Alex was quiet, unknowing what to say or what to believe.

Allan hugged Alex, and Alex returned the gesture. "We can talk more later," Allan said.

"Can I take my new truck for a drive?"

"As you wish," Allan said. "Careful on the road."

***

Alex took his car out for a drive, to lose himself in the joy of his new gift. He turned on the radio while on the road. A song called, "Mama Said," began to play.

Alex exhaled, overcome with emotion, and parked his car in the nearest retail parking lot to take things in. He listened to the song, the memories impacting him, and he thought of what his father had told him about his mother's humanity.

Alex's hand reached for his cell phone and he dialed his mother's number.

"Hello?" Anna answered.

Alex's words got caught in his throat, and what came out was raw with emotion. "Mom... I'm sorry for being harsh before. I didn't mean it."

Anna's voice on the other end was calm but firm. "Happy birthday, Alex," she responded with a hint of resignation.

"Guess what?" Alex continued, smiling. "I'm going to college. USC."

Anna was quiet. Alex waited for her to say anything.

He was scarcely about to share more, when Anna interrupted him.

"If you go there, you're no longer my son."

The line went dead.

Alex was frozen in defeat, sitting in his truck. His mind was a mess, but he remembered he promised his father to drive safely. After taxing his mind of agony, it took all he had to focus on driving home.

***

Allan watched his son pull up in the driveway. Alex was in tears. Allan opened the passenger side door and sat beside his son.

"Dad," Alex sobbed, "she says if I go to USC, I'm no longer her son!"

Allan placed a hand on Alex's shoulder, offering silent support. "Family is complicated, son," he said gently. "Sometimes we have to navigate through the mess before we can find clarity. But this... going to USC and making your mark there? That's something she should be proud of."

The weight of Alex's emotional turmoil settled into a heavy silence as Allan sat beside him in the new truck, watching his son struggle against tears. It was a rare moment of raw vulnerability for Alex, and Allan knew it was time to offer more than just words.

Allan continued, choosing each word carefully, "Sometimes families hurt each other without meaning to. Anna's response doesn't reflect your worth or her dreams for you—I think it's her pain talking."

Alex sniffled, wiping his eyes with the back of his hands. "But Dad, she's my mom. I want to fix things."

Allan nodded, understanding the depth of his son's longing for reconciliation. "I know you do," he said softly. "And it's admirable. But sometimes we have to step back and heal ourselves before we can help others heal."

He paused, allowing Alex a moment to digest this advice.

"Your mother has her battles, just like you and me. It's okay to distance yourself for a while so that you don't get hurt more in the process," Allan continued. "You focus on your dreams at USC. Show them what you're made of."

Alex nodded slowly, the confusion still evident but softened by his father's wisdom.

"Also," Allan added, "let me handle communications with her for now. It might be best if you and her get this some space and time to heal."

Alex looked up at his dad, gratitude shining in his eyes, and exhaled with relief.

"I'll think about what you said," Alex replied.

***

Alex was much more refreshed by Monday, proudly displaying his new truck at school, drawing the admiration of many classmates. Among them was Marty, a girl Alex had harbored feelings for. She asked him for a ride, and against his lingering reluctance due to personal burdens, he agreed.

Stepping out from under the weight of his troubles seemed momentarily possible as Alex and Marty escaped together into the freedom of the day. The absence from school on that particular Monday became a shared secret.

In the days that followed, Marty and Alex found themselves inseparable. One afternoon, curiosity prompted him to ask about her middle name.

She revealed it was, "Amy." Intrigued by this new facet of her personality, Alex asked if he could call her, "Amy," instead.

She smiled warmly at the proposal and consented without hesitation. "Of course," she said, "from now on, you can call me Amy."

From then on, Amy became more than a nickname; it was a bond, a shared piece of their individual identities that melded into something unique and personal.

This small change in how she was addressed signaled to Alex and Amy that their connection was more substantial than he initially realized.

Later that night, Anna was alone in her study.

She picked up her phone and called Allan.

"Have you talked Alex out of going to USC yet?" she asked.

"No," Allan replied over the phone. "And you are not going to try."

Anna started yelling at Allan, calling him so many names.

"That school is where you cheated on me with Beth! Remember?" Anna shouted.

Allan answered, "Do you know how many years ago that was? Yes I was young, I know now that was wrong, but even so, you and I were dating then! We weren't married, unlike what *you* did, having another family with Tom behind our backs."

"If you don't talk Alex out of going to that college then, then fuck you!" Anna shouted.

The line went dead from Allan.

Anna let her phone fall and started to break down in her computer chair. She couldn't stop crying. She cried all night long in the study. For years, Anna had felt like a mess. Her life, her thoughts, her feelings...her whole happiness was a train wreck. She was feeling guilty about what she had done to Allan and the kids. She kept asking herself what she had been thinking? How did she not realize things would come to this? She kept grabbing her hair and pulling, asking herself why she hadn't known better to foresee these consequences?

Alex was on the computer at home, signing up for his first

college classes. His phone rang—it was his mother, Anna.

He checked to see if his father was nearby. When he saw he wasn't, Alex answered softly.

"Hello?" he asked.

"Alex?" Anna said, "Is it ok if you and I could meet somewhere today? If not, sometime this week?"

Alex spoke softly and nervously. He wanted to see his mother, but he knew he wasn't well in her presence. He knew he was already pushing himself by answering the phone for his mother.

"I'd rather not. I'm not ready for that yet." Alex replied. "I'm sorry."

***

The days went by, and on the day before Alex would leave for college there was a soft knock on the door.

Alex answered. To his shock, there stood his mother, Anna, offering a birthday card to him.

"Please," she said. "Take it."

Alex took the card, just as he heard Amanda, his younger sister, running up the stairs to her room. She slammed the door and cried.

"Is that Amanda?" Anna asked in the doorway.

Alex could see his mother was breaking down behind her eyes.

"We'll handle it," Alex answered as respectfully as he could.

Anna nodded and left promptly, exchanging an unspoken good-bye with Alex.

Alex shut the door and opened his birthday card.

The inside read, "I will always be there for you."

***

Amanda didn't want to talk to anybody that same day. The only one she would let in was her big brother, who was leaving the next day for college. It was going to be Amanda's first year of high school. She wanted to be one of the cool girls. Alex tried to tell her she shouldn't have to worry about those kinds of pressures in high school, and what was really important was looking out for herself.

Amanda didn't say much back. She didn't know about Alex's advice. What did he know about being a girl in going into high school?

The following weeks to come, Alex was loving college life. Especially the parties. They offered an escape from his sorrows and the tension at home. Sometimes he felt like he could forget his home altogether. The girls loved Alex. He was so much fun to be with. He hosted a lot of the parties in one of the dorm rooms right off campus.

In high school, Alex never got bad grades, but come the first semester of college, Alex got his very first D, much to his father's displeasure. Allan promised he would pick his grades back up, so his dad gave him the chance and still made his truck payments–but he wanted to see good grades on his report card.

***

Later on in that semester, as Alex was relaxing at his dorm, the doorbell rang unexpectedly.

Alex opened the door and was shocked again. His mother,

Anna, was standing there, shaking intensely. Her car was parked right outside, and in the passenger seats were all three of Alex's sisters whom Anna had with Tom.

Anna was pale as plaster, and mortified.

"Mom?" Alex asked. "Are you all right? Is something wrong?"

Anna struggled to speak. "Yes," she said. "I don't know who else to go to. It's Tom. I let him back in..."

Alex froze sickly.

Anna continued, "He's been raping the other daughters for two years now! Behind my back! He's in jail," she broke down in front of him, gritting her teeth. "No bail this time!"

Alex fought with an eruption of so many mixing feelings, and he looked at his mother as maturely as he could muster. "Mom, you need to go tell Amanda all of this. You didn't believe her before, and now you do."

"It's not just that, I...I-I *walked in* on him assaulting Amber! I saw it with my own eyes! I was never so angry in my life!" The tears spilled down her face. *"Two years!* Please, can you watch your three sisters for a while? I have to go and talk to Amanda. Your dad and your sisters will be here soon. Your father is going with us so that Amanda does not run off or do anything stupid."

"Yes, Mom, I'll watch them for you," Alex replied.

Alyssa was now eleven. Amber was nine, and Allison was two years old.

Allan and Amanda pulled up shortly that evening. Amanda

ran up to her big brother and hugged him. She missed him so much.

Allan beckoned Amanda calmly to come with him and Anna back into the car. Amanda followed in, and they drove off together to go talk someplace quiet nearby.

Minutes when they were on the road, Amanda couldn't hold in her rage anymore.

"This is all your fault, Mom!" she barked.

"Amanda," Alex said.

Amanda continued, "You had to have two husbands and all kinds of kids with that monster!"

Alex made a turn beside a pond just outside the dorms, and parked.

"Amanda," Anna said very calmly. "Can we go and sit over there so we can both just talk?"

Anna, Alex, and Amanda, walked and sat together at a bench.

"Amanda, I'm so sorry for not believing you about Tom," Anna said, going pale again and her eyes glazed over. "I'm ashamed. Ashamed I betrayed everyone. Ashamed for what I thought I saw in that awful man, and just...ashamed I lied and kept it a secret. I don't know what I was thinking. I should have known better. And I'm ashamed I didn't believe you...my own daughter. I chose that monster over my own daughter."

Amanda didn't say anything. But much as she was angry, she still wanted her mother back. And here she started to see her mother again, as she once knew her.

"Can you forgive me, Amanda?" Anna said.

Amanda remained silent.

Allan spoke up softly. "Amanda, I know the past few years have been turbulent. We could all tell ourselves, 'I would never do this,' or 'I would always be better than ever doing that.' But that can be any of us. We can all do wrong. And sometimes, we all do. Even things we never thought we'd ever do. We never know what kind of situations life is going to put us in. And we never know how we're going to react, or what unwise opportunities we might try and take. We shouldn't. But any of us can fall short. And right now, your mother wants to do a good thing. She wants to come clean for everything."

Amanda's eyes moistened.

"And if we love her," Allan continued, "And if she's sincere, we'll respect that."

Amanda sniffled and finally said. "Yes, Mom. I forgive you."

They hugged tight and cried together, Allan joining in.

"I'm so sorry," Anna said again. "I walked in on Tom attacking Alyssa. Now he is back in jail where he will stay for good."

At the mere mention of the details, Amanda began shaking and ran back to her father's car, calling Allan and Anna to hurry her back to Alex's dorm.

Arriving back, Amanda took Alyssa outside for a walk with Anna and Allan. They walked to the park that was only about one block away from Alex's dorm.

Anna and Allan watched from a safe distance out of earshot while Allysa sat with Amanda and told her everything that Tom, her dad, had done to her. She then asked Amanda if that's what happened when she was there. Amanda went on to tell her what Tom did to her.

The two girls spent what felt like hours talking together. They cried, they laughed, bonded, and walked back to the house, hand-in-hand.

From that day on, Amanda knew her sisters needed to be with their mom and her dad, Allan. She wondered if they could get back together again and if there was something she could do.

She didn't know they were already talking about moving into a guest house nearby the dorms.

# Chapter 3

Anna and all three girls moved back in under Allan's house.

That same night, Anna and Allan were talking in private in the backyard. The grass in the yard was still so short and young. Only sapling trees along the fences.

"What made you go and get married and have more kids with somebody else?" Allan asked. His tone was direct but calm. "I just can't understand why?"

Anna looked at the grass as she stood beside him.

"You told me after we had Amanda that you didn't want any more kids. You forgot how many kids I wanted. I told you before we even got married and you were all for it then. But after Amanda it was like you changed your mind."

Allan winced.

"And that's when you got with Tom?" he asked.

Anna sighed. "I had told you before we got married that I wanted seven kids. I wanted seven because seven was my lucky number. We had two kids, and Tom and I had three girls, and..."

"Wait?" Allan asked. "Why didn't you just try to talk to me

about it? Even if I forgot you could have reminded me."

"I was afraid you'd say no," Anna replied. "At the time, I didn't want to argue with you. I was afraid you would shoot it down and I'd feel betrayed. But you were so happy. I didn't know how to bring it up and I was thinking about how to bring it up, but...then I met Tom."

Anna buried her face in her hands, feeling shame. "When I got pregnant with him, I didn't know what I was going to do. I felt like I couldn't go back, but I was also getting the more kids I wanted. Looking back I thought I could live two lives and be happy. I knew it was wrong to cheat, but I just...got carried away and swept up into something that made me happy...at least until it all came tumbling down."

Allan only listened, with both concern and care.

"But living two lives isn't living. It's not loving," Anna went on. "Maybe love itself just had enough with me playing my games. I'm so sorry, Allan."

"Anna," Allan said. "I'm sorry I forgot. Listen, though, we should be able to communicate. We shouldn't have to fear just talking to each other. We didn't talk, now we're looking back at the roller coaster it put us through."

Footsteps approached from the house. Anna and Allan looked back to see their daughter, Amanda glaring.

"This happened," Amanda said. "All because you didn't want more kids, Dad? Mom, only because you wanted seven kids, all over some stupid *lucky number?* You messed up all five of us kids' lives for your own reasons!"

27

"Amanda, go back inside," Allan said.

"So us, the children, pay for your mistakes!" Amanda persisted. "Both of you! Now we have to live life like this right here, right now! You messed me up so bad! Well now let me tell you I've made a mistake too!"

"Amanda?" Anna asked.

"What 'mistake?'" Allan asked.

Amanda broke down crying. It took her a minute before she could speak again. "Dad, you know Robert, my best friend?"

"Yes?" Allan asked. "Amanda what is going on?"

Amanda answered in a fit, "Two months ago, we had sex and today we found out that we are going to have a baby!"

Allan and Anna looked at their daughter in shock.

"What are you two going to do with a baby?" asked Anna.

*** 

The days that followed were uneasy.

Anna was contemplating the news of the baby. Had she really messed up this much by her affair with Tom? Was the drama going to spread down the generations? She was thinking about how to fix her family and make amends, but she was worried she had already failed.

After one week, however, Amanda came to Anna alone.

"Mom?" Amanda asked. "You still really want seven kids right?"

Anna sighed, "Not now, Amanda."

"No Mom, just listen," Amanda said. "Why don't you and dad adopt our baby?"

Anna looked back up at Amanda, "What?" she asked.

"You can be the baby's mom and dad. And that will make six kids. Robert and I will always be in the baby's life still, but...you get it, right?"

Anna's eyes moistened. "Amanda," she said with a smile, "that is very clever."

She hugged her daughter for a good long while. "Let me talk to your father about it. We'll let you know what we decide together."

"Ok. Please say yes," Amanda said, relishing the hug.

"It might take us a few days," Anna told her. "We need to think about this carefully, just the same."

***

Another week later, Amanda came to her mother and father as they were discussing the possibility of adopting the new baby. Amanda was holding a folder in her hands from the doctor's office.

"Mom! Dad!" she asked excitedly. "You want to know the sex of the baby?"

Anna and Allan regarded each other and exchanged a silent agreement.

"Yes," Allan said.

Amanda grinned bright and gave the folder to her parents. They opened the folder seeing images of an ultrasound.

"It's a son!" Amanda said.

Anna bounced in her seat and grinned. "I can't wait to have a son after all these girls!"

Amanda's eyes opened wide and her jaw dropped excitedly. "You decided to adopt the baby then?"

Allan smiled and nodded.

\*\*\*

The week before Amanda was due, Anna went down to Amanda's room to check on her daughter. Amanda stood up to greet her mother, and her water broke. Anna and Allan drove Amanda to the hospital right away.

Hours later, Anna was holding baby Andrew in her arms. She was so thankful.

Andrew even looked a lot like Allan.

After three more days, Andrew came home with his adoptive father and mother. Amanda chose to stay at her boarding school.

When Anna got home with the new baby, Amber didn't like him. She thought it meant her mother would now be gone all the time, like she was with Allison.

Anna reassured Amber that she will never go anywhere for her job again.

Alex came home shortly after the delivery. He didn't know the truth about Andrew, as the secret had been kept from him.

Alex picked up Andrew and was sitting on the couch holding him fondly.

"Hello, Andy. I'm your big brother, Alex. I promise you I'm going to teach you everything that a big brother gets to teach their little brothers."

Andrew held onto Alex's finger as they regarded each

other. Alex grinned proudly and then looked up.

"Hey, has anyone seen Dad?" he asked.

"He said he was going to run an errand or two this morning," Anna said. She checked the clock and saw it was an hour past noon.

Shortly thereafter, Allan unlocked the front door.

"There he is!" Anna said.

Allan regarded Alex and smiled, "Welcome home, young man," he grinned. He then shouted for the whole house to hear, "Now then, I have a big surprise for all of you!"

"Allan?" Anna asked. "What have you been up to?"

Allan offered passage through the front door to the van and said, "Come and find out. You'll love it."

All entered the car and Allan drove a short while into another part of town.

"I'm doing this because...look at my family," he said proudly. "Ok, everyone, close your eyes."

Each family member closed their eyes, each exchanging a curious glance.

Minutes and several turns down several streets later, Allan counted from one to three.

"Open your eyes, everyone," he said, "And look to your right-hand side."

When their eyes opened, they all yelled in excitement. There, sitting on a nice corner street, was a newly constructed three-story house.

Huge tears gushed from Anna's eyes and she covered her

31

mouth. She turned to her husband. "You did this for us?!"

Allan held up the keys with a nod.

*** 

It took the family five days to move into the new house completely. There was even a guest house connected to it. Alex, having his own apartment near his school, took his own belongings with him. Amanda also went back to boarding school as she wanted. Her grades were improving immensely. Alex's grades were passing, even though they weren't the greatest.

On Andy's first birthday, Anna and Allan's parents came over as well—the grandparents of their children. All generations had so much fun that day.

When Andy was sixteen months, Anna was not feeling well and went to the doctors. She found out that she was pregnant with baby number seven. When she got home Allan was right there asking if she was pregnant again. Anna told him yes. Her family is almost all here now.

Anna started to show around three months into the pregnancy.

As the doctor was doing the first ultrasound on her baby, he said with a nervous chuckle, "Oh boy, Anna. You are really not going to like this."

"I beg your pardon?" Anna asked.

"You are going to have baby number seven and baby number eight. You are pregnant with twins!"

"Twins!" Anna exclaimed beaming happily. "I hope you can tell the sex of the twins very soon!"

That evening when the whole family was together at the dinner table, stood up. "I have really good news. I found out about 1-week ago that I am going to have twins."

Each jaw from Anna's kids dropped and eyes flashed opened.

"Twins?" asked Amanda.

Anna grinned. "I have baby number seven and baby number eight inside of me. I hope that I have boys because you girls kill me with all of your fights you guys try to put me in the middle of it."

Christmas arrived as the twins' room was being put together, Anna got Allan a new case for his work. The case came with a note that said, "To the best husband, father, and best friend. I love you."

Allan almost cried when he read it. Enclosed in the package was also a new wedding ring.

Allan got Anna the prettiest ruby ring earrings, necklace, and she fell in love with them. Each one of the kids got them stuff for the house and the girls got their dad a pen set for his office.

They also gave their mother a necklace with a pendant strung on it that said, "Mom," on it.

In the middle of the gift openings, Alex asked his girlfriend, Amy, to marry him.

She said yes.

Allan looked at Anna and said, "I knew he was going to pop

the question."

Anna smiled big and opened two more small gifts. "Now the moment we have been waiting for. Alyssa, Alex. You open this one, and Amber, Allison. You open the other."

She handed the gifts respectively.

"Who are these for?" Amber asked.

Anna chuckled and said, "Just open them."

Alyssa and Alex were already opening the first one gift. Inside the gift was a piece of paper with the name "Adam."

Amber and Allison opened the second. Inside was the name, "Anthony."

Alyssa smiled in excitement. "The twins are boys?"

Anna nodded excitedly! "What do you all think?"

Everyone loved the names.

The girls were so happy; they yelled so loud that everyone heard them for blocks away.

In the weeks that followed, Anna had to take it very easy. She was going to be due any day. Before the end of January, the boys wanted out.

Allan drove Anna to the hospital and she was put in her own room. The doctor came in and let her know they would take the babies in the morning if she could make it that long. The boys were waiting for their moment.

Both boys were out at sunrise. Anna was exhausted and fell asleep for the next three hours.

When the doctors woke her up, the first thing Anna asked was if she could see her boys. They told her she would get to see them after she was taken back to her room. Then they would bring the twins for her to see.

Days later, Anna and her new baby twins got to go home happily. Andy just loved the twins. He would try picking them up, so Anna would put them in Andy's arms, and he would just be so nice to them. He was always kissing the twins, always wanting to help his mother.

***

Three months later after the twins were born, Alex and Amanda were coming home from their respective schools. Alex told Amanda that his and Amy's wedding was sometime in July, news that Amanda was ecstatic about.

Alex pulled up into the driveway and Amanda went in first while Alex stayed behind to unpack the car. The first thing she did was go to her room and put her things away.

The house was oddly quiet. Anna nor Allan had greeted her when she came home. Amanda looked around and noticed all the children were asleep.

Amanda went to her mother's room to check on her. As she was approaching the door, she could hear her mother crying very hard. Amanda ran inside and her mother asked her "Mom? What's wrong?"

Alyssa walked into the room, uncomfortably watching as her mother was crying.

Three minutes later Allan came into their room, presumably to say hello.

Before he could breathe a word, Anna started yelling at him

35

furiously.

*"Get out of my house!"* she roared.

# Chapter 4

Allan called his wife the next day and she answered her phone. For a few minutes he heard only crying. She tried to talk, but she was still very upset.

He knew why.

"Anna, I know you're very upset," he said. He sighed in defeat. "I'll call you back later ok?"

He hung up and called Amanda's phone.

It went straight to voicemail, and he was certain Anna was telling the children.

At the tone, Allan recorded his message to Amanda.

"I'm truly sorry," he said, his breath shallow. "Please, can you keep an eye on your mom for me?"

***

Amanda had innocently missed her father's call, but after hearing his message she was confused, then felt a sinking of anxiety inside her. She went to her mother's room and sat down next to her mother.

"Mom," she asked. "How are you?"

Anna was in bed, crying. It had been hard for her to talk

and communicate the past two days.

"Mom, I'm here if you need to talk to somebody," Amanda said. "Please."

Anna looked at her with a red eye, wet from heavy tears.

"Your father left all of us for another woman," she said.

Amanda frowned in defeat, as her worries were confirmed.

"She doesn't have any kids and she is younger than me."

"What are we gonna do?" Amanda asked.

"I never want to see him again," Anna sobbed. "Why did he have to do something stupid?"

At those words, Amanda scoffed, a flood of unhealed rage spilling in her emotions.

"Well look at how long you were with Tom. And you let him rape me!" she started hissing through her teeth. "You didn't even believe me until you walked in on him raping Alyssa! How could you do that to dad? So now I just guess it's his turn to do it to you!"

Anna screamed into her pillow.

Amanda continued, "Mom, you have two babies who need you now. Andy too. So get up and get your head out of your ass. Get out of bed, go take care of your kids because I'm leaving too! And nobody is going to stop me from leaving! I go off to USC this year and I'm going down there to look at a house. A one-bedroom rent. Right down the street from Alex."

Amanda watched as her mother sobbed shakily and nodded. She was old enough now to recognize her mother was simply empty. Defeated, running out of tears to cry, and pain to feel. "Okay," she breathed, stammering. "That's fine. You'll be here tonight?"

"Yes," Amanda replied. "Why?"

"Because I need you and Alyssa to watch the smallest kids. I just need to go out for a while. I'll be back."

***

Anna got up, took a shower, and got dressed and kissed her children goodbye, telling them she would be back within four hours.

However, that evening, Anna left on an airplane at night, back to Vegas to her old house there.

When she walked into the house, the following morning she felt an odd sense of control and stability. It was just her in a house all to herself.

After two hours of being home, Anna felt she needed to escape in peace. She had no strength left. She felt she had failed too many times. Allan had been unfaithful just as she had, and her children were in disarray emotionally.

She called Amanda again.

"Mom? Where are you!" she asked. "There's no one watching us!"

"Amanda," Anna said. "Tell your father he needs to move back home. I'm never coming back again..."

"What?!" Amanda exclaimed.

"Goodbye."

***

"Okay I'm on my way now," Allan said, receiving the frantic

39

call from Amanda. He wasted no time grabbing his keys and headed out the door to his car. "How are the other kids?"

"They don't know anything right now," Amanda said. "Please get here soon, Dad."

Allan was out the door and walking to his car. "I'm coming right over," he said.

Afterward, Amanda called her brother Alex to let him know as well.

Alex didn't answer his phone.

"Come on, pick up! Pick up!" Amanda said. She tried again to no avail.

***

No one knew yet that Amy, Alex's girlfriend, had also left him for somebody else.

Alex had started drinking.

After he had showered to tried to get sober again, he checked his phone and saw the many missed calls from Amanda. He sighed, knowing there must be more trouble now. He called her back, taking a seat. He was so tired.

"Where have you been?" Amanda barked on the phone.

"Sorry I was in the shower," Alex replied. "What's up?"

"I've been trying to call you for half an hour!" Amanda yelled. "Dad cheated on Mom! We found out two days ago! Mom's left the house, I don't know where she is now, but she said she'd never coming back; I don't know what that means!"

"What?" Alex asked. "Did she take the boys with her?"

"No, but you really need to come home!" Amanda said.

"Dad's here too, but he has to work, and someone needs to watch the kids!"

Alex trembled, twice devastated. His mind was threads from falling apart. "O-okay," he said in a stammering voice, words still slurring slightly. "I'll be home in three or four days. I have to get ready for the last day of school. Until next semester."

Amanda sighed. "Right. When you go back, can I stay there with you? At your house? I'm through with this place myself. I have my own life to live."

"Yes, yes," Alex said. "You're coming over to USC, that's what I remembe," he took a moment to compose his thoughts.

"So much has changed here," Amanda said. "Home doesn't feel like home anymore. Anyway, sorry I yelled, I just didn't know what you've been doing."

"I know," Alex said. "Sorry."

"All right," Amanda said. "I'll see you soon, Alex."

***

Allan walked into the house just as Amanda was hanging up with Alex. She hugged him, in spite of everything. The twins also came to hug Allan.

"Thanks," Amanda said. "I'll make dinner. Just watch the little ones a while, please."

Allan nodded silently.

Amanda hugged the twins briefly and then went to the kitchen to cook.

Even as he kept watch on the kids, Allan kept on calling Anna, concerned for her safety.

41

She didn't answer her phone. There wasn't even any ringing, showing her phone wasn't on. Maybe not even charged.

***

In the days that followed, Anna changed her hair color. She was going by a new name. She changed as much about herself as she could, so she wouldn't have to recognize the turmoil she'd been through.

One day as she was hanging some new clothes in the closet that she had just bought, the doorbell rang. At first, Anna acted like nobody was home, but feeling on guard, she walked to the window and peeked out of the curtains and between the shutters. Allan was waiting by the door.

He had found her, but she didn't care anymore. Not about apologies, not about anything. She was done with him.

But she watched as Allan left something in front of the door, then walked back to his car and drove away.

When the coast was clear, Anna opened the door, checked her surroundings, stepped out and found Allan had left her a letter.

She picked it up, opened the envelope and read the message, which had no greeting nor farewell at the end:

"You have 6 months to get your ass back home with all eight of our kids. I said I was sorry. Besides, I did even have sex with her. We may have kissed, but not more than that. Again, I'm sorry, but you need to come. Our daughter is going to college this year. There is also something very bad going on with Alex."

Anna took it all in. Once before, as many times already, life hit her and she questioned what she was doing with herself.

An hour later, she was back at the airport.

***

When Anna arrived home, Allan took her immediately to USC to see Alex.

Once Alex had finished his classes for the day and returned to the dorms, his parents were standing in front of his door.

"What are you guys doing here?" Alex asked, concerned as he was surprised. "Amanda said Dad left, moved out, and then Mom was never coming home."

Allan replied with compassion, "Amy called and told me what was going on with you two. Alex, can we come inside?"

Alex relented and welcomed both his parents into his dorm. As they entered, Alex's composure broke, and angry tears began to flow.

"Why did she have to cheat on me?" he sobbed. "With my roommate? My best friend, even?!"

Allan winced, "Amy said you cheated on her."

"No Dad, I would never do that!" Alex shouted. "After I've seen you and mom cheating on each other, after all that did to me? No! Never!" he sat on the couch and spiraled into a full breakdown. "Mom had another husband in Vegas years ago, kept it a secret from us for years! I could *never* hurt Amy like that."

Allan listened, while Anna took in his words with as much grace as she could.

"Amy also said you are drinking really bad, is that right?" Allan inquired. "She said she couldn't take it anymore. What does

43

she mean by saying you were drinking?"

Alex sobbed in reply, his face drenched. "I like to drink after I'm done with school, and I work very hard every single day! It helps take the stress off! I try to drink responsibly at least!"

"Alex," Allan tried to say.
"I'm twenty-one years old. I can drink a couple beers if I want to drink, right?! I'm working very hard at school and a job! I hardly have a life! So Hell! What if I want to drink?"

Allan listened and asked, "Did Amy try to talk to you about it?"

Alex broke down all over all. "I wish she had!" he answered. "All she had to do was talk to me! If she had just talked to me about it I would have listened! But no! She cheats on me and then lies to you that I cheated on her!"

Anna started to cry as well. She knew she'd done wrong in her past. Being back near USC did not help her focus, but Alex was more important to her than her past now. She questioned why she had even tried leaving again. Trying to leave her life behind, even her children. She wondered how to live with herself when she kept making the wrong decisions in her life, questioning her own loyalty and love.

It seemed whenever she tried to escape, love itself had something to say about it. It always seemed to find her and catch her, convict her, and bring her back, leaving her wishing she could have done things differently.

She began to have impressions in her mind and in her heart, wondering if things might have been different, easier, better, if she and everyone in the family had simply talked. Communicated, understood. No secrets, no lies, nor the consequences they brought.

But it was too late for the best now. Anna only hoped she could stave off the worst.

"Alex," Anna said. "Just be strong. I know I don't set the best example, and I don't know if you'll believe me because of so many other things I've said and done to you. But right now I just want to say I'm proud of you."

Alex looked up, stunned.

"In spite of everything you've been put through, you always do your best. Please, just...don't give up. Whatever happens to you, Alex, don't let go of your standards. I don't want to see you sink or...become any kind of man less than you are."

Anna sobbed. Allan looked at Anna as well, gentle approval behind his eyes.

"You have four days left of school," Anna continued. "Then you'll be off for the summer. Just focus on finishing this semester as best you can. Then maybe look into taking care of yourself before the next one. Amanda will be coming up with you too. You both can look out for each other."

Allan nodded to Alex in agreement. "We can't control other people," he said. "But you can control yourself. Look at your hands, Alex and flex your fingers. Make fists. Look at your hands and remind yourself, those are yours. You have a smart mind and good heart. You have control over yourself, and you can always ensure you can do what's right and best. Even if sometimes others fail you."

Alex calmed down and took a moment to breathe, nodding.

"Do as your mother says," Allan told him.

\*\*\*

Alyssa was starting high school that year. Amber started junior high and Allison was in fourth-grade. Andrew was turning three-years-old, and the twins, Adam and Anthony were almost a year old.

That summer went by too fast.

In August, Alex and Amanda were getting ready to leave for college together. Anna helped to make sure everything went smoothly for their living situation, especially when she heard where they would be staying.

"Alex wants to rent a house right off campus?" Anna asked. "Not be in the dorms?"

"We thought it would be good if you get it for us," Amanda explained.

"Who owns it?" asked Anna.

"The college owns the house and they rent it for off-campus housing. We just think it'll be great that we're in the same house. More comfortable, and we can keep each other company there."

\*\*\*

Anna considered the request and talked it over with Allan.

Confirmation for the house rent arrived by email before the semester began. The siblings would be set. Rent for the house was sixteen-hundred dollars.

There would be two other men staying who would help

with the rent.

Two days before Alex and Amanda would leave for USC together, Anna met with her son.

"Your father and I have paid for your rent for 6 months, Alex," she told him. "Your rent is now $400 between you and Amanda."

Alex winced quizzically.

"You paid only half our rent?" asked Amanda.

Anna nodded. "Your half. For six months. After that six months is up, I will stop your rent."

Alex winced, posed to protest or negotiate further.

"Alex," Anna went on, "I know you said you've been working very hard to make ends meet, and that's gotten you to drink. I know you're trying to drink responsibly, but it's a slippery slope. This is so you can get a  head-start on your finances, so when the six-months is up, you'll be in a better spot. Do you both understand?"

Alex sighed, brows sagging, nodded. "Yes, Mom. Thanks."

Anna smiled and then went into talk to Amanda separately, finding her packing clothes.

"We got the house," she said.

"Yes!" Amanda cheered.

"But," Anna proceeded. "Allan and I have paid Alex for only six months, though we will be paying for your stay for only your first year."

Amanda began to frown.

"After that, you must pay her own rent, just as Alex did

when he started."

***

When Allan came home that night, both Amanda and Alex approached him.

Alex began by saying, "Hey Dad, thanks for the rent, but... can I have longer? I don't think it's fair that Amanda gets one year of rent and I only get six months."

Allan responded, "What your mother and I say is what's happening."

Alex went on, "You're giving Amanda a full year. You didn't give me a full year of rent when I started."

"I understand," Allan went on. "But please understand your mother and I feel we are already being very generous now. And you still have a home here, with your siblings. We need to take care of this place too. We've been paying a lot and carrying you all, and its been long enough. You're both grown up and need to pay your own bills."

"But Dad," Amanda began to protest. "Is it that much more?"

"You both are capable. You both need to embrace your responsibilities and help yourselves."

"But we can," Amanda said.

"Then you already have more than you need from us," Allan said. "Alex has been there, we're helping him get back on his feet again. We understand as much as he does that it's a hard adjustment, so we always have your backs. Both of you. It's just that time for you to start your own lives. That may come with it's share of responsibilities which *are* very important. Remember it will also come with it's liberties too. That's something to look forward to, right?"

***

Two days later, Amanda was going to leave with her brother for college. Alex drove and Amanda rode as a passenger.

"I don't know how this will work out," Alex told her before they arrived, "with the other two guys I mean."

"What *do* you mean?" Amanda asked.

"Just try to keep a distance from them please," Alex said. "They're older besides and I'm just concerned for your safety. You know."

Amanda listened.

"I truly hope you will let me know if they try anything with you," Alex said.

"I'm not a kid."

"Maybe so, but you're still my younger sister. I can't help but care."

"Trust me, if they try anything funny, I'm not having it. And I *will* let you know."

Alex smiled and exhaled in relief. "Music to my ears."

***

After half-a day's drive, Alex and Amanda arrived at USC in the evening.

49

They entered the house, immediately sensing the difference of how homely it was opposed to the dorms.

The two other students had already settled in. Alex introduced himself and his sister to the others, who introduced themselves as Mark and Jacob. Amanda went to settle into her room to get a head start on unpacking while Alex, Mark and Jacob conversed and got familiar with one another. Their conversations were off to a good start, until Amanda walked back out to the car for a second bag of her supplies. When she was out of earshot, Mark and Jacob admitted to Alex that his sister was very pretty. Alex saw in her faces and body language how impressed they both were.

"Remember," Alex charged, his demeanor much more deflective. "She is my baby sister, so don't try anything with her."

***

Amanda managed her first day college, becoming acquainted with the campus and reviewing each class's syllabus. When she made it back to the house, Mark was there studying. He bid her welcome, asked how her first day of college went—informing her that Jacob was still in class. Amanda happily let Mark know she liked her first day. After leaving her school supplies in her room, she went into the living room to relax, leaving Mark to continue studying. They started small talk and then continued getting acquainted with each other through friendly conversation.

Minutes later, Alex arrived at the front door.

"Hey, what are you too doing?" Alex asked, a tinge of

50

suspicion in her tone.

"We're just sitting here and talking," Amanda reassured her brother. "Getting to know each other. That's it."

Alex nodded, sensing Amanda was safe.

Amanda went on. "College is different, but I liked it. I had to make it to my first class at 8:30."

"11:00 AM for me," Alex said, setting his school supplies down. "And I'm there till 2:15 in the afternoon."

"I was off at 1:15," Amanda said.

"I see," Alex said, checking the calendar on his phone.

"Yeah, and since I get out so early, I'm thinking that will give me plenty of time to look for work too today. I'll be holding off my studies until tomorrow."

Alex frowned at his phone as he continued checking his agenda. "Well I have another class in a few hours, and it's over a little after 5. At least it's only two days a week. As for the rest of the week," Alex continued, pocketing his phone, "When I'm not getting R and R, I'm going work in a lawyer's office."

"Really?" Amanda asked brightly. "You're finally doing work as a lawyer!"

"As an intern," Alex said with a smile. "I'm planning to, anway. Some offices are offering internships and I want to take advantage of that. I'm still thinking about which office. I plan to finally get my bachelors at the end of this semester. After that, I'll be working on my Doctorate, and I'll be able to start working in the courts."

"That's great!" Amanda grinned.

"Yeah. Well, let me just shower and get ready for that next class."

Alex left for the restroom.

"He seems like a great brother," Mark told Amanda.

"You don't know the half of it," Amanda said with pride.

After a thoughtful silence, Mark spoke up again. "Would you like to go and eat dinner with me tonight. I'm thinking of getting burgers and fries, nothing fancy.

Amanda thought a moment. "Yeah," she said. "I would really like that."

***

Alex did not like the idea of Amanda going out alone with Mark, but Amanda convinced him she would be all right.

Mark was a very nice young man. He and Amanda were both the same age. Amanda loved the food at Mark's favorite restaurant. Afterward, while there was still some light outside, they went for walk in the park, then sat down on the bench and talked more while the sun went down and the day cooled.

While they were conversing, Alex called Amanda on her cell.

"Hey, where are you? You all right?"

"Yes, Alex, I'm fine, I promise. Mark and I decided to go for a walk after dinner, that's all. We're at the park."

"Ok, well be home soon. You know you have class in the morning.

"Alex, come on, you've been like this all day with me, I'm

52

fine. I appreciate you're looking out for me but you're being too much now. I'm adult."

"Just the same, please come home, ok?" Alex said. "I'm really nervous."

"Just stop it, we're just out here at the park talking, ok? We'll come home no later than nine o'clock promise."

"Amanda," Alex began to object.

Amanda just hung up the phone, upset with him.

***

Amanda returned with Mark at nine o'clock as she promised.

Even after dinner, Amanda and Mark spent time outside on the front steps, without Alex knowing, and talked even more. They didn't come back inside until one o'clock in the morning after which point, they said their goodnight.

The next morning, Amanda and Mark both had to be at school at the same time, so they agreed they would both go in one car this semester to save on gas.

Back at home it was only the girls and babies without Alex or Amanda. Andy was growing fast and seemed to be getting into everything. His climbing skills made it difficult to keep him contained over the gates they set up.

On the girls first, day of school at the end of that summer, Allison got into a fight. Anna was called and had to take all three baby boys with her, a job in itself.

When she got to the school, Anna called the office from the

car and asked for Allison to come to the car and watch her three brothers.

Allison walked out to the car and got in the car and her mother didn't say a word to her.

Anna was informed of what Allison had done did to the other child, and was even allowed to see. When the talk was over, Anna's could only frown, her face was ripe with disappointment for Allison. She went back to the car and looked at Allison sternly. Allison didn't say a word back, exercising defiance.

When school was over, Allison was told to help watch the boys.

Anna went to her room to call Allan and let him know about what happened today at Allison's school. Afterward, Anna went downstairs and put them in the the boys in their pen in the nearby room adjacent to the livingroom.

"Allison," Anna said. "Come and sit down here so we can talk. What is going on at school?"

Allison set down and, arms folded and frowning. "First off, I didn't start the fight, the other girl did."

"Did you see the face on the other girl after the fight?" Anna said. "Did you see what you did to her?"

Allison looked away, pouting.

"I truly don't know about you right now, do you understand that? You are grounded."

"Until when?" Allison asked.

"Until I say you're not grounded anymore," Anna said. "I don't want you going anywhere, and you're giving me your cell phone."

"But Mom!"

"No. It's mine, until I give it back to you. I have already called your father and he is mad at what you've done."

***

When Allan arrived home, he gave Allison a similar lecture. Allan even asked for her phone, to which Allison responded, "Mom has it already!" after that, she went back to her room and slammed the door. Anna yelled at Allison not to slam the door ever again.

The next day when Allison went to school her. When she came home, she marched straight for her room to close herself in. The whole door however, was missing.

"What's going on here?" Allison asked.

Anna walked in. "I removed the door to your room. It's in my room until you're not grounded anymore."

"The hell?!" Allison exclaimed.

"And that attitude doesn't help your case," Anna replied sternly.

Allison stormed into her room yelling strings of accusations against her mother.

She wouldn't even come down for dinner that evening, refusing to eat with her mother, so when dinner was done, Allan told her, and Allison ate her dinner alone.

***

Now back at USC, Amanda and Mark had been spending a lot of time together.

When Alex got home from college one afternoon, he asked where Amanda and Mark were—they weren't home. Jacob, the other roommate, told him they were on their date.

No sooner, Amanda and Mark walked in the door. Alex turned around right away.

"A date?" he asked them both. "Really?"

"Alex, not now," Ameanda told him.

"Yes now! You are too young to be dating!" Alex yelled.

Mark, Amanda, and Jacob all quizzically looked at Alex.

"And I told you I didn't want you to mess around with the other roommates!" Alex said.

"I am in college just like you are!" Amanda said. "I'm *not* too young to be dating! And you didn't tell me you didn't want me 'messing' around with the other roomates. You said for me not to let them try anything with me! They haven't!" Amanda started marching to her room. "Honestly, Alex, I'm more afraid of having to deal with you when I come home, lately. Not either of these two!"

***

In the morning, Amanda called her mother before school. She told him about Mark and Jacob, explained how polite and reserved they had been, and how much she loved dating Mark, but most importantly, Amanda asked if her mother could talk to Alex. His behavior was very concerning, and she felt unable to get though to him.

Later after Alex's class, Anna called her son and confirmed the details with him.

"Alex," Anna told her son, "You should leave Amanda and Mark to themselves. Amanda says nothing is going on, she is being treated well, and I'm concerned you're becoming too controlling. As long as Amanda is safe, she deserves to make her own friendships."

Alex thought over his mother's words and relented. "Okay," he said. "I'll leave them alone. I promise."

Allan's voice came over the phone then appreciatively. "All right. Good on you, son."

"Dad?" Alex asked. "Yeah, I overheard you and mom. Just wanted to come say hi. It's good to be vigilant of your sister's safety, but don't overdo it. Amanda sounds like she's ok for now."

"Right," Alex said. "Thanks Dad."

***

That same day, after Alex came home, Amy arrived.

Just as Alex was walking out the door to head to his evening class, he saw Amy and promptly went back into the house. Amy followed him to the door and started crying because she missed Alex a lot, telling Alex she dropped out of school and wanted him back in her life. Alex told her to leave the house before he called someone.

Alex didn't go to school that day–his mind in pain from reopened scars.

Amanda came to check on her brother after Amy had left with her meltdown.

"Amy dropped out of school to come and see me," Alex scoffed. "Honestly, she should just focus on her school, but she

57

dropped out to see me? No, we broke up, after what she pulled. Why would she miss me!"

***

Allan was going to see Alex and Amanda this coming weekend.

He never asked Anna if she wanted to go with him.

Allan left Friday night and Anna asked him where he was going.

"I'm going to see the other two kids," Allan said, Allan kissing the other kids goodbye. "I'll be back Sunday."

"You didn't tell me."

"No I didn't," Allan said. "Because you still intend to leave us."

Anna was quiet. Earlier this week, she had said it was true, and she could see Allan was upset with her about it.

"You still want to leave this family and start over," Allan went on, huffing a sigh. "But Anna, I've been seeing how much you care about your children. But in spite of that, you tell me this is only until the Alex and Amanda are stable. I share my house with you, I even continue to share my money with you, the same bank accounts, as a sign my trust. In spite of everything we've been through before. But I can't keep up this roller coaster. When we married, we said we we would be a team. We trusted each other to be loyal to one another."

Tears began to fall from Anna's eyes, as she felt convicted all over again.

"Not loyal some of the time, but all of the time. But I can

58

see that's not what you want. You're not willing to uphold your end. So I'm going to see our kids. I know I'm on borrowed time with you, so I won't stay attached...and I suggest if you really mean what you say about leaving us, you don't stay attached to them. When you leave, Anna, follow through with what you say. Don't say one thing and then do something else. Too many hearts get broken in this world when people do that."

Allan left through the front door, and Anna went up to her room and started crying.

***

That weekend, Allan stayed with Alex and Amanda. They all had so much fun seeing their father again. Allan really liked Mark–they had so much in common and they spoke for hours about their interests.

Meanwhile, Sunday morning, Anna got the twins ready to leave.

She had packed the car on Saturday night after the kids were sleeping. She left in the car with the twins, leaving Andy, Allyssa, Allison and, Amber home–Allison still without her cell phone.

Amber came in and asked Allison if she would like to use her phone until their parents got home, to which Allison agreed. Allison used the phone for everything except to call her mother– still wanting nothing to do with her.

In the afternoon, Anna, nor the twins and Andy were home. None of the girls knew what was going on.

Allan didn't come home until after 1PM that day.

Alyssa went up to her father.

"Mom and the twins with you, Dad?" she asked.

"No why?"

"She hasn't been home all day and neither have the twins. She didn't even say where she was going."

Allan ran upstairs and opened Anna's bedroom door. He looked into her closet and her drawers. Everything was gone.

He opened the twins' door and everything in that room was gone. Anna took both cribs, the clothes, and the toys. He went back into the living room.

"When did she leave?" he asked Alyssa.

"Around eleven I think."

Allan sat down on the sofa and called Anna's phone. It went right to voicemail without even a ring.

"What's up now?" Allan left his message. "Where are you and the twins and Andy?"

He must have called her a million times that night. Alyssa tried calling her too, but got the same thing.

***

Allan called Alex and told him to call his mother.

"Tell her to call me right fucking now!" was what he said.

Alex called her and he got the same thing. No answer.

Amanda tried as well, with the same result. She then asked Mark if she could use his phone, which he allowed.

The phone picked up, "Hello?"

"My father said you, 'need to call him right fucking now.'"

"Who is this?" asked the woman on the other end.

"It's your daughter! Don't play stupid with me!"

She then heard another voice on the other end and it was a man. Amanda could tell he was a bit older.

"Hello, miss, is everything all right?"

"Who are *you!*" Amanda asked.

"I'll explain, miss, I'm sorry. We got this phone from a woman who was living in a house across from us. She said we could have it. We're still trying to figure out how to use it and get a new number for it."

Amanda replied, "Was that woman with twin boys?"

"Yes, ma'am. She hired a moving truck, I think about two or three men were helping her move out about three or four hours ago."

"Is she still there?" asked Amanda.

"No, ma'am she left with the moving truck recently and gave us this phone. Just said she was moving on with her life and then left. Is Anna your mother?"

"Yes! Did she say where she was going?"

"No, ma'am I don't. I just think I heard one of the movers driving the truck say something about a three hours drive 'up north.' Me nor my wife knew Anna had any other family."

***

After that call, Amanda got her phone, called her father and told him the whole story.

Allan cried as she was telling him. He dropped the phone and put his head in his hands and cried.

Alyssa came in, having overheard everything. She hugged

him, crying with him. "You got all of us, Daddy," she kept saying. The other girls came in, following her example.

"We love you," Alyssa went on. "I promise you, Daddy, I will never leave you, never. Never in my whole life! I'll stay with you, Daddy."

Allan hugged his daughters. "I just don't understand why she took the twins with her and not andy. Just the twins," he sobbed again. "I still love your mother! This is my fault. I should've kept letting us heal. I was too hard on her last Friday, what I said...even before that I shouldn't have even gone near that other woman even for a bit! Even if it wasn't 'as bad,' it wasn't right of me! It doesn't make me any better. But Anna was coming back! She was coming back! And I messed it up!"

He sobbed again, his tears drenching his face. "I still love her! It's just hard to learn how to trust somebody again who messed up. It's so hard to trust a person again!"

***

Determined to find Anna and the twins, Allan got a very old friend of the family to ask their daughter to come and stay with Alyssa and help her babysit. He said he would pay her very well for doing this.

Allan chose not to contact to police, at least for now. He refused to believe Anna would truly kidnap the twins. He believed they were all safe, and that he had time to try to find them all and make things right.

Before he left, he gave the girls five-hundred dollars for anything they needed, while he was gone and left to go find his wife.

He stopped at Anna's old house, and met the elderly man there whom Anna had given her old phone to. Amanda had called him back and asked if he could meet with her father. After introductions, they went out to a sandwich shop where the edelman man explained in more detail what he saw and knew.

"Anna knew me and my wife for a while. She didn't have any kids with her at that time. She told me about two months ago that's she would pay us a lot of money if we would take care of her house, so she showed us her house, gave us all the keys, even said we could could eat there and if we needed anything we could call her. She was gone a long time, but we got paid. We might have called her a few times asking how she was doing. She said she was fine, never told us what it was about though. We had to wonder, but she said make yourself at home. Then She came back about yesterday with the moving company, paid us a little extra, and that was it."

"And you don't know where she went?" Allan asked.

"Like I told your daughter, no, I only heard something about a three hour drive. The only other thing—and I'm sorry I forgot about this part when I was talking to her on the phone—she mentioned something about going ot Scotland or Paris."

Allan's head went into his hands and he started to cry hard.

***

Anna was neither in Scotland or Paris.

She was moving to Idaho where she intended to raise the twins alone.

She had a bought another house there, already and was just waiting to get there with the boys. It was an easy to drive twins slept a lot of the way. While there had been a stop three hours from Anna's old house in Vegas, it took her two days to get to Idaho.

When she arrived at last in her car, one day ahead of the moving truck, she began to unpack the car with the twins. She was exhausted, and was having trouble handling both the twins and the laundry and toys. She could nearly have cried at the thought of setting up the cribs with how tired she was.

A man walked over and offered to help her, if she was comfortable with that. Anna was so tired she said yes and thanked him.

He helped her unpack the car, carrying everything in while Anna handled the twin boys. When he was done and Anna had observed he set everything where it needed to go properly, she thanked him.

"You didn't have to do this," Anna told him.

"I normally wouldn't impose," the man said. "But you looked so worn out with your two boys, I was worried you looked ready to pass out."

"Much do I owe you sir?" Anna went on.

"Nothing, I could see you needed helping hand, that's all. Would you like me to put the cribs back together for you?"

"You've already done so much, thank you. I can do that myself."

"All right. My name's Drake."

"I'm Anna," Anna answered. Even though she had legalled changed her name, that's how it came out. "Thanks again, I won't keep you. Your wife may get mad at you for being here too long."

Drake bowed his head sadly, pausing gravely. "No wife, ma'am."

Anna saw sorrow overcome him.

"She died two years ago with our only son," Drake said, regarding the twins. "My son was seven months old. She was driving while drinking and...got herself killed with my son. So no, I don't have anyone who will get mad at me."

Anna was stunned a moment. "Oh I'm so sorry," she said remorsefully.

***

Drake was allowed to set up the cribs afterall while Anna fed the twin. After dinner, she put them both to bed with pacifiers and walked back into the living room. Where Drake was waiting for her.

"I was going to ask," he said, "If you're hungry, I can pick you up something to eat too."

"Thank you, yes," Anna thanked him softly. "If you're sure."

Drake nodded. "Ok, I'll be back in thirty-minutes. Mexican food all right with you? The Mexican place down the street has the best burritos that I have ever had, with rice and beans."

"Oh, I love Mexican food," Anna replied. "Do they serve chips and salsa too?"

Drake smiled, "I'll be back with burritos, and lots of chips and salsa."

"Here," Anna stopped him. "Let me get you some money to get us some dinner. Since you've helped me a lot already even picking up the food, I'll pay. Oh, and some tea with lemon? In a large cup with lots of ice?"

She gave him fifty dollars.

"Use whatever is left over to get yourself anything you want and then keep the change."

***

After Drake came back, they sat down at the fireplace to eat and they started talking.

"Thank you once again," Anna said. "The moving truck will be here tomorrow with the rest of my things."

"If you like, I can help you more tomorrow then."

"Oh, you've already done much," Anna tried to object.

"I have nothing better to do," Drake said. "It must have been a long road with just you and the twins, driving up here all alone, without a husband."

Anna winced. "How did you know I...don't have a husband?"

Drake caught his tongue. "Sorry, ma'am, I didn't. I assumed. Just that no good-hearted husband in my book would let a woman like you drive up here alone so long with twins. Not without some extra help. Not unless maybe he was in the military or...I don't know. I'm sorry. What happened to him?"

Anna shook her head. "It's a long story, but we went our separate ways."

Drake nodded. "I see. I'm sorry."

He was quiet for a thoughtful moment. "How do you feel about... dating a younger man?"

Anna smiled but shook her head, and answered, "I don't know about dating right now."

***

Alyssa was still home with other kids, when her father called on her cell phone.

"Have heard anything from your mother?" he asked.

"No, dad. Did you find our anything?"

As she was talking, the house phone rang, and Alyssa put her father on hold to answer it. Amber answered it first.

"Hello?" she asked.

"Can you give the phone to your father?" Anna asked. "I want to talk to him for a minute."

Amber excitedly mouthed to Alyssa, "It's Mom!" before she said, "Daddy is out looking for you. Where are you?"

Anna only responded plainly. "Tell him to go back home. He will never hear from me because he will never find me."

After that, Anna hung up.

***

Back in Idaho, Anna and Drake were becoming very good friends. The twins loved him too. Anna was there with the twins when she said she needed to make a call. In private, she called her oldest son, Alex, just to check on everyone briefly another time.

"Hello?" Alex asked.

"Alex. It's Mom. How are you and everyone?"

67

"Where are you and the twins?" Alex asked.

"I already told your sisters the same thing."

"No! Where are you and *my* twin brothers?!" Alex shouted.

Anna couldn't take the pressure. She hung up.

***

Allan got a call from Alex, promptly thereafter and told him he had heard from Anna.

"Did she call you with any number," Allan asked.

"Yes. She tried from an unknown number but I have an app on my phone that revealed it. I think she's in Idaho."

"Give me the exact number, Alex. I'll find out for sure."

"Ok. Dad, Amanda says Mom means to disappear with the twins. I'm really scared I'll never see my baby brothers again. I don't know about Mom anymore, as far as I know, this is it between me and her. Just please make sure the twins are safe."

Allan sighed, feeling the rifts in his family tearing again. "I'll do I can," he said.

***

Allan was able able to trace the number. He was driving to Idaho, when he phone rang: there was no caller ID. He stopped his car alongside the road and picked it up.

Anna talked to Allan for almost a whole hour, but Allan felt his pleas to make things right weren't reaching his wife.

"Anna, I love you Anna so much!" he said. "I still don't understand why you would take off like this and leave me alone with the kids, but take the twins with you. Please, let's work this out."

"I've made up my mind, Allan," Anna said. "Yes, I wanted the twins, and you can keep the other kids. The twins are still babies and nobody can take care of them like I do."

"Anna, please, at least tell me where you'll be living. Let me know your number or some way to get a hold of you so can see the other kids."

"I don't want to see the kids. And you won't see the twins ever until they turn eighteen–years-old."

Anna hung up, leaving Allan broken, feeling powerless to save this. After a moment of painful contemplation there in the car, Allan finally decided Anna was gone.

And he saw only pain in front of his every next moment.

***

Anna was was spending a peaceful night with the twins in her new home, when a knock came at the door. She got up to answer, hoping everything was okay with Drake.

She opened the door to see Allan, who stormed inside, walking past her.

"Allan!" Anna screamed. "Allan what are you do doing!"

"Getting my kids!" he boomed.

"No!"

"You tried to run away with our kids, and leave us all behind. I won't allow that."

Allan carried both twins with him in the car. Anna was screaming in a panic, trying to open the doors of Allan's car, but Allan had locked them. Allan drove off, before Anna could do anything to stop him. Anna chased him down the street, seeing red, but his car drove off leaving Anna stumbling in the dark road, falling in the mud just down the street from her house, crying, shaking, traumatized.

Later that night, Anna called the cops, and Allan was the one arrested for kidnapping the twin boys.

# Chapter 5

Anna arrived at the jail house to pick up the twins and told the cops just to let Allan out of jail, so long as he left for home immediately alone. She then looked for a different place to live.

Drake was besides Anna frequently, expressing his compassion. He was still getting to know the full story. Regardless, he just wanted to do what he could for Anna, after these difficult few days. After everything that transpired between them, Anna knew she had tried to handle things her own way. Even though Allan had been the one to be arrested, she knew now she could have faced the same.

Thus, she started her divorce case, and sent the papers to Allan's workplace.

***

Allan started to cry when he saw the papers arrive at his work office. He questioned if anything he could have done different could have saved their marriage and kept their family as one. After taking a deep breath and keeping his composure, Allan stopped himself. He kept telling himself, "What was done is done." Anna was gone now. Maybe the twin boys now as well.

Maybe Anna had the right, by now.

He signed the papers and enclosed a personal letter:

*Anna,*

*You can have custody of the twin boys. I hope you will allow me and the rest of our children to see them, but I understand if I've destroyed that opportunity. I'll send you $900 a week for now to help. Then I'll send it once a month. I hope you find your happiness. My world is gone, but I take responsibility for my actions that contributed to everything falling apart. In spite of everything, I will love you to my last breath is taken.*

*Allan*

\*\*\*

Anna got Allan's letter in the mail four days later along with the papers. After reading, she started to cry, and sat down that night and wrote him a letter back:

*Allan,*

*I don't know if you'll understand, but if not, it's ok. I was feeling like you didn't love me anymore, and I hated you for that. I know I tried to run and*

*disappear, and even before that, I also take*
*responsibility for everything that came before. I*
*know we want to be together, but maybe we just*
*don't deserve each other. But you will always be*
*here in my heart. No matter what I may have said*
*in the past—or believed—I'll never stop loving you*
*Allan. Thank you for the twins, I promise to take*
*the best care of them for us both.*

*Love, Anna.*

Alex and Amy got back together that the end of autum, though Allan was skeptical that it was a wise choice. He especially wasn't keen on the idea of Amy staying at his own home until she could get back on her feet—as she and Alex had requested together. Amanda requested to move back in too for her added security. She and Alex withdrew for the semester and would continue classes in the spring for Amy's sake. Allan didn't like any of it. It complicated a lot, including the rent situation for the on-campus house, and all the money that had been paid in advance. He relented in spite of his reservations.

Amy agreed to listen to Alex during her stay, as his father owned the home.

Amanda assisted helping Amy and Alex move in during the soonest weekend she could afford.

That Christmas was a somber one for the family, gray and dull in contrast to last year's.

Three days afterward, Mark called Amanda, to see how she was doing with the family, to which she answered things felt slow, and empty, especially after Christmas.

"I wonder," Mark said. "Could I drive up to see you sometime?"

Amanda asked her father who was nearby working in the kitchen.

Allan nodded. "Mark? Yes, he come by anytime."

Amanda smiled, happy to see Mark had earned her father's trust.

"He says yes, anytime," she answered.

"Tell him thanks, for me!" Mark said. "Would it be ok if I drove by New Years Eve? And if I could take you on a date that night?"

"I'd love that," Amanda said.

"Be sure to be dressed up extra special, to your liking," Mark answered with joy. "Because we are going to paint the town red!"

***

Over the next three days until New Year's Eve, Amanda bought the most gorgeous dress for herself, despite her father entrusting her with his bank card and telling her to not, "Go crazy."

She tried it on and loved it, eager to impress Mark when he arrived.

Mark arrived at the house at sunset on New Year's Eve. Amanda heard Allan answering the door for him downstairs as she was setting her shoes on.

"You look very handsome," Allan said told Mark, which summoned a cloud of butterflies for Amanda.

He brought Mark to meet Amanda upstairs, and Amanda was stunned before she could even great him. Mark was dressed in the finest suit she could have expected, with nice shoes to match. And when Mark set his eyes on her, she could pleased to see how he looked wonderful and equally smitten by her.

"Wow," Mark said. "You...you just look so gorgeous."

Amanda hadn't even noticed that her father had prepared a high quality camera. He took several pictures of them together.

Before leaving, Mark let Allan know that they would not be home until tomorrow morning, much to Amanda's surprise. She could see Allan's face wince with concern.

"What?" Amanda's brother, Alex, said. "No, you'll have my sister home by 1 in the morning, no later."

Allan only let another relenting smile.

Then he gave Amanda a long, loving look in her eyes. Amanda sensed he was looking at his daughter and simply taking evering in. Concern, fear, joy. Memories, longing, acceptance. She thought she could see so many things before her father's eyes. Emotions and thoughts wrapped up together and mixing and playing before his sight with great impact.

"All right," Allan said. "See you both tomorrow morning."

\*\*\*

Amanda had so much fun with Mark, dinner, and then dancing all night long at the the local dance hall.

At midnight, he kissed her for the first time, as fireworks set off. Amanda was already falling for Mark, but once they met for that first kiss, their lips could not separate.

Mark then had the limousine drive them to the fanciest local hotel Amanda knew—he had booked reservations days in advance. As soon as they walked into the room they couldn't keep their lips away from each other, nor their hands off one another.

They made the most passionate love that night, losing themselves in one another, and they fell asleep when the sun was coming up, and then made love one more time before leaving the hotel.

Before they left, they made love one more time.

When they pulled into the driveway Alex was outside waiting, looking displeased. The only thing he said to Mark once Amanda was out of the limo was, "You can leave now."

Allan came outside and asked Mark to come into the house, however. He wanted to talk.

***

Mark sat down next to Amanda this time they were holding hands. Alex was seated in a far chair in the corner, with a frown and furrow in his brow.

Allan closed the door, but wasn't able to breathe a word before the phone rang. Allan asked Mark and Amanda to excuse him while he answered the phone.

"Hello," spoke a man's voice on the other line. "May I speak to Allan?"

"This is Allan," Allan responded. "May I help you?"

"Yes, sir. My name is Drake. I live across the street from Anna."

Allan's brow furrowed with concern, feeling a strange sinking in his gut.

"Anna? Is she all right?" Allan asked.

"Yes, sir, she is," Drake answered. "But the twin boys are very sick in the hospital. I think you should come now. They are in the children's ward. Anna won't come home for nothing, either."

Allan held his breath and replied, "Thank you. I'm on my way."

***

It wasn't just Allan who went. Everyone on left that day on the plane exccape Amanda and Mark, who stayed with Andy. Hours, that same day, they landed in Idaho and met Drake at the airport. From there, he Drake led them to the hospital, and then to the room where the twins were. They recgonized Anna's crying several doors away even before they entered.

Anna was sitting and crying beside the twins who where each in an ICU.

Allan took Anna in his arms tenderly.

"Look," he told her comfortingly. "Look who all came to see you and the twins."

Anna looked at Drake in surprise.

"You called my husband?" she asked.

Allan's eyes watered when he heard what Anna called him.

"Yes," Drake said. "You can kill me later for it. Right now your family really needs you."

Tears spilled from Anna's eyes and she simply cried and Allan's shirt, letting him hold her in his arms, surrounded by her other family.

"Where's Amanda and Andy?" she asked.

"They're at home," Alex said. "Amand and her new boyfriend are watching over Andy."

Anna reached out with her arms to embrace her family.

Many hugs were exchanged, and many tears shed over the twin boys.

Allan got up afterward. "Here. I'm going to try and get a hold of the doctor. You all want to stay here and keep your mother company."

All nodded, except Alex. "I have to get home. I need to prepare for the next semester."

He got many quizzical stares from his family.

Alex started walking toward the doorway. "Please keep me informed on the twins. I love them."

He left the room—too suddenly.

Allan looked to Anna, an understanding look in his eye. "Why don't you go for a walk. Maybe get some coffee." Those were his words, but both he and Anna knew it was time to confront Alex.

Anna got up and walked out of the room and followed Alex toward the reception area.

"Alex?" Anna asked.

Alex looked over his shoulder briefly and turned his back to her.

"Alex, please, I need to tell you something!" Anna insisted. "Alex please!"

Alex spun around with a snarl.

"What fucking right did you have to take the twins with you and leave all of us behind again?!" he boomed. "Fuck off, Mother! I don't need you anymore!"

"Alex."

"No! Why did you just take the twins? The way you left all of us, and now *you* need us? Of course, *your* twins are sick, so *now* we matter?! Remember, you left all six of us. We didn't leave you!"

Anna's arms were shaking and her jaw was rattling from her head.

"Alex, listen to me."

"I won't. You're a bitch, Anna!" Alex said. "I hate you! Just go back to *your* twins. I got my brother Andy at home. He needs a mother too, so bad he cries at night for you. But I don't think he deserves you. Maybe one day he'll thank me for protecting him from people like you."

Anna tried to speak, through her quaking body, but her voice was silenced. Her thoughts were seized in her mind. She couldn't even move her feet to follow Alex as he walked toward the Hospital exit.

***

Alex called his father and told him he was going to a motel for the night. Allan let respected Alex's wishes–though he was disappointed with what he had told Anna. The next morning, Alex got on the plane and went back to the house alone.

Anna couldn't help but take the time to feel incredibly hurt by what Alex had said to her.

Fortunately, the following day, the twin's condition had improved and they were moved to another room. The doctor ordered they were to stay there in the hospital for the next two days. She also told Anna she would be 'eighty-six' if she didn't go home and shower and eat something and rest for 6 hours, and that she didn't want to see Anna before that.

Anna did so, and went home where her other girls were waiting to hear news of the twins. Anna walked in to see Alyssa and Amber in the living room.

"The twins are doing better," she said in her weak voice. "The doctor says they just need a couple more days."

Amber smiled with relief. Alyssa however frowned on the couch.

"Who do you think you are mom?" Alyssa said. "Leaving us the way you did. That was so wrong of you!"

Anna was exhausted, and already very broken inside. "Not you too," she said deflectively.

"You only wanted the twins!" Alyssa sneered, getting off the couch. "Why, Mom?!"

Anna stood her ground, feeling cornered, wounded, and ready to fight or run.

"Do you hate all of us? What did we do to you?" Alyssa stomped up to her mother and shouted in her face. "What mother?! Tell me now!"

Anna's hand swatted Alyssa across the cheek. "You won't talk to me like that ever again!" she replied.

Alyssa started to cry, holding her cheek. "I hate you, Mom!"

"Then I hate all of *you!*" Anna yelled, crying as well, speaking through turbulent thoughts. "It's not like you wanted me around anyway. You all just want to be around your father. You don't need me, you don't deserve me, so I left you kids with your father! Well, if you kids hate me, why the fuck are you in my home. Get out all of you!" her shouting became vehement screaming. "Just get out of my life! Leave my home and leave me alone! Go and get your father and take him with you kids! I don't ever want to see you kids again!"

Amber got up and took hold of her sisters, alarm. "I'm sorry you feel this way mom," she said, calmly.

Anna slapped Amber too after those words. Amber had meant to be opened to her mother, but after that strike, Amber new it was time to leave.

"I hope you are happy with yourself now, Mom!" Alyssa shouted back as they left the house in a hurry, both her and Amber were nursing their faces.

When Anna had cried at home a while, she went back to the hospital, disregarding the doctor's orders. She just wanted to be with her babies.

Allan was walking out of the Hospital with Alyssa and Amber, who were crying. Anna could have shoved past them all indiscriminately. She didn't even look Allan in the eye, let alone Alyss and Amber.

"Anna," Allan said as she pressed on to the room. "Anna, I'll always love you!"

Anna didn't want to hear it. She went back to the room expected to just be able to sit with the twins.

Two cops were waiting in the room when she arrived. They promptly arrested her for assault.

As the cuffs were binding her wrists, all Anna could do was cry and scream and shout.

*"I hate you Allan!"* she wailed. *"And the kids!"*

*** 

Drake went and picked up Anna from jail the next day.

He was driving her home when he asked, "What happened?"

Anna was quiet, but felt like she was a trainwreck inside. "They had it all planned out," she said. "Allan was part of it too, I know he was."

Drake didn't inquire anymore. He questioned if he had done the right thing called Anna's family. All he could say was, "I'm sorry."

When Anna arrived home, she walked up the steps and found a letter from Alyssa. She bent down to pick it up, but was trembling, afraid of what it would say. Afraid of being torn up again with words.

The letter read:

*Mom,*

*I'm sorry that I am mad at you. I didn't mean
everything I said. When you left us you left me
there to raise your kids. I'm still a kid myself. So
until you want to see me again, Goodbye. I'll let you
make the call.*

*Love always,*
*Alyssa.*


Anna sat there on the porch thinking about all eight of her
children, mourning the loss of six of them. In spite of Alyssa's
words, in spite of Allan's promise to love her always, she couldn't
take the ups and downs anymore. She new all she had now were
the twins.

In five days, they would be a full year old.

***

Drake and Anna started dating in the days that followed.
They both liked each other, but
Anna was having a hard time trusting him. She wasn't sure how
she felt about the possibility he would become new family. She
was tired to turbulent family bonds, and wasn't ready to take
chances.

She kept teller herself it was ok. They weren't going too
fast, and taking things good slow. This time if there was trouble,
she knew she could stop things there.

That weekend, Anna celebrated the twin's first birthday.
Drake and his nieces were allowed to join. Two women who had

been coworkers with Anna were welcome arrivals as well. Both brought their babies, totaling five together.

The twins boys had started walking three days ago, and all the attendants of their party were found it adorable as they tried walking about.

Drake got the twin big wheels as birthday gifts, which they loved immediately. For the rest of the party, that was all they would play with.

One of the Anna's coworkers got the twins a swing set for outdoors. When spring and summer came, it would be ready. Anna was eager to see how the twins would like the swing.

***

First day of Spring arrived and Anna took the twins to go outside. Drake was seated on the bench set up in the back yard. He wished her good morning, and Anna replied in turn. She then went to play with the twins in the backyard.

"Anna it's all right, let them play together," Drake bid.

"I want to play with my sons, and that's what I'll do." Anna responded.

"You're not a kid, they are," Drake said. "They can play alone with each other. You can sit here with me."

Anna looked at Drake wardinly. "They are my kids and if I want to go outside with my boys I will. There is nothing you can do about it."

Drake nodded, raising his hands as a sign of relent.

"Thank you," Anna said. "You nor any man will ever tell me what to do, how to do it, or what to say. I'll handle things."

Anna went on to play with the boys outside. Drake left her house quietly that hour and went home.

***

Drake didn't talk to Anna for three days.

In the middle of the week, Anna went to Drake's house to check on him. Drake answered, and when Anna asked if he wanted to go dancing that night if she could arrange for a baby sitter, Drake told her, "No," and closed the door on her face.

Anna grimaced and shouted through the door that she was done with him.

Drake opened the door again and told her to leave.

After that, Drake would not even look over at Anna, even if they were neighbors.

Anna wondered if the twins missed Drake when he wouldn't come over anymore.

She told herself she was doing well to reassure herself. Anna had everything she needed. She didn't need a husband or any family other than the twin boys.

***

Back at Allan's house, the Alyssa and Allison were fighting all the time. Allan couldn't keep them disciplined was feeling like he couldn't keep them disciplined.

One day after he tried to get them to go to their rooms and not talk, Alex called on the phone.

"Hey Dad, how is everything going?"

Allan groaned. "Don't you want the girls for a week or two?"

"Are they really fighting that badly?" Alex asked. "I know that this is hard on you but it's all got to workout. They will work out and they will be best friends by the end of this."

"I hope so. I know you want to take your little brother again for the summer," Allan sighed. "I'll try and figure something out till then. And I know Amanda and Mark are coming home in the summer too.

Allan hear Alex sigh over the phone. "They can use my apartment this summer if they want, I guess. If it gives them peace from the girls."

"I might take the girls to do something this summer in august. I don't know, maybe we'll visit Rome for two weeks."

***

The next workday, Allan was sitting in his office. Spring was on its way out and summer was coming, and he was trying to prepare for the trip to Europe with his daughters. Shortly before he clocked out, his cell phone rang and he answered it.

"Hello."

"Allan? It's Anna."

Allan suppressed an exhausted sigh.

"What do you want, Anna?"

"Are you busy right now?" Anna asked.

"It's a quiet day at the office and I'll be clocking out soon."

"Allan..." Anna spoke in a weeping voice. "The boys and really miss all of you. We want to come home. For good this time."

Allan shook his head to Anna's plea. In his mind, this was the last thing he wanted to deal with. "Anna, I really hate to say this to you, but hell no, you cannot come home. You've lost your home. I can't handle this back and forth game anymore. I'm physically sick from going back and forther between, 'I love you,' and 'I hate you.' And after everything that happened back in Idaho, I don't think the kids feel safe with you anymore. This is not healthy for us and it's especially not healthy for the kids."

Anna was crying on the other end. "I know," she explained. "I tried to live alone, like this. Just me and the twins but the days go by and I realized I can't. I just want to come home. I miss you, and I still love you Allan."

"I've heard that before," Allan said, "But this is a cycle. It needs to be broken."

"Allan please, I'm sorry. What, are...are you dating another new woman? I'm not letting her go for you or anybody else!"

"Anna you have had so many chances to come home," Allan told her. "Now we are all doing our best here and we can't afford any rollercoasters. We have to finally let this go."

***

Amanda and Mark showed up at home. Alyssa and Allison were both so happy to see their sister again.

Andy came running and jumped into Amanda's arms, and she hugged him dearly.

"Where's Alex?" Andy asked.

"He's coming in about one hour, all right, big guy?" Amanda said. "He's coming to get his little buddy. Andy, you can have my bedroom for the summer is that all right with you?"

"All right, I guess so," Andy replied.

87

An hour later, Alex arrived just as Amanda said. Andy yelled so loud and happily and Alyssa ran downstairs and jumped into Alex's arms. Alex was so happy to see his sisters and his little brother.

"I have all my things ready to be put into the car!" Andy told him.

"Good, my guy," Alex said. "I'll be spending the night here though, and then after eating tomorrow we'll head on over to my place."

***

Andy, Alex, and Alyssa all went to sleep in Andy's room that night.

Early the next morning after 5AM, Andy woke up excitedly, and Alex and Alyssa grabbed cups of coffee to go.

They hit the road not long afterward, which allowed they to arrive at Alex's home prompt in the afternoon.

Alyssa and Andy ran right into the house to find out that the other roommate, Jacob, had moved out and took everything from the house. They opened up Mark and Amanda's room as well. Everything was gone out of there too. The only thing left was a plate that was dirty.

There was nothing Alex could do but call the cops on Jacob. Fortunately the school had all of his info and they gave it to the police, who looked for him at his paretn's home. Jacob's parents told the police they had not seen or heard from their son since the day he left for college.

The following day, Alex had to call Amanda and Mark and

let them know what had happened. They had scarcely made the call, when there was a knock on the door–it was the police, along with a moving truck driver come to return everything Jacob had stolen.

Fully relieved, Alex thanks the police and helped move everything back into the house, whilst Alyssa called Amanda back to let her know the situation.

Amanda instructed that her things should just be moved into the closet–she would take care of them when she came back before school started again.

***

A few days later, Anna showed up at Allan's house with the twins–Amanda was housestting. She had driven all the way from Idaho and was intent on moving back into the house.

Amanda called her father at work to let him know what was happening.

Allan showed up promptly thereafter. He was only pulled into the driveway when Anna went running over to him crying, pleading to let her move back in.

"Anna, I'm sorry. But we went through this," Allan said. "We've tried this too many times, and it's time we need to uphold our boundaries. I don't need you continuously coming back and then leaving the kids the way you do again and again. It's not good for us. You need to go somewhere else."

***

Anna got back into the car and began a long drive back to the house she left in Vegas. She was so mad at Allan for denying her to return. Deep inside, Anna felt guilt and the pain was so immense it felt she couldn't breathe. She missed her family, regretted her decisions that caused them to lose their trust in her. But she felt she couldn't take the defeat. She had to have a resolution somehow. But maybe it wasn't possible anymore. Anna was fractured in pieces. It took all her strength to stay focused on the road during the long drive to Vegas. Half the time, she felt she droned on autopilot.

Anna arrived in Vegas and found an elderly man resting on her porch.

Though he was a stranger, Anna paid him to help her unload her car and move back in. As a further thank you, Anna allowed the man, who introduced himself as Ronnie, to stay in the guest house.

The days that followed, Ronnie found the living arrangements with Anna agreeable. He and Anna got along well, and he was very respectful of her and the twins.

"If you would like Ronnie," Anna told him one evening, "You can live here always. This way I can go back to work again. I'll pay you for the babysitting boys."

Pleasantly surprised, Ronnie thanked Anna humbly. "How much would you pay me?" he asked.

"You'd be the boys Nanny, essentially. I'll pay you $650 once a week. Now you have a job and a place to live. You can help with bills and food, and you don't have to pay rent."

Ronnie was stunned at this offer, and graciously accepted.

Anna believed their paths crossed for a reason.

For the rest of that summer, Alex, Alyssa and Andy helped their father, Allan, to look for a new home. The family had decided it was time to find another place to live, as the house Allan had bought so long ago felt it carried too many haunting memories.

Alex researched the market and found an amazing deal. The house had three stories, eight bedrooms, and four bathrooms, including a back house that was two stories tall. Alex talked to his father, Allan, who liked the idea of moving there.

Allan arranged a meeting with the seller that weekend to discuss purchasing the two houses. After said discussions, the seller let Allan know she would finalize her decision on his offer by the following tuesday night.

Tuesday came, and the seller approved Allan's deal, and wished him and his family a brighter new future in their new home.

# Chapter 6

Allan and the kids started packing their own rooms the next day.

In one week, Amanda had her room sorted, and the next week Andy's room was done. Mark assisted as well, much to Allan's gratitude.

Days before they moved out completely, Amanda found her father looking at the facade of the house from the front yard as the sun set. She met him and asked if he was ok. Allan nodded and expressed that he intended to give Anna some of the money from selling this house.

"I know she has my boys," he said, longingly, eyes glazed over with bittersweet memories. "She's working again and will have a babysitter, but I still want to make sure she'll be ok and that my boys grow up knowing they have our support and our love too. I know Anna's having a hard time with me turning her away. I just hope one day she understands why I upheld these boundaries."

Amanda held her father, supportively, to which he wrapped his arm around her.

"I know could have let her back in," Allan continued. "But who is to say she wouldn't do it again?"

"Can I say something, Dad?" Amanda asked. "Maybe we wanted to see her. All your kids. I know you were upholding your boundaries, but maybe it would have been better to talk it over first with the rest of us? To see how we felt about it?"

All bowed his head. "I'm sorry, Amanda. Maybe, but I also saw how Alyssa and Amber were affected too. And especially Alex. I'm worried the pain keeps going back and forth and escalating. Every time we try getting together again, things get worse. Especially last time at the hospital visit."

***

Anna called Allan that evening while he was relaxing in his bedroom. She asked if he could send her some money. She had just started working again but could use the extra help.

Allan answered her, "When the house sales you will get a part of that money."

"You're selling the house?" Anna asked, surprised.

"I've already sold the house, we're moving in someplace new," Allan said. "I'll send you $500 until the money comes in, ok.?"

"How much did you sell it for?"

"I'd rather keep that confidential," Allan said.

"Allan, do you not love me anymore?" Anna's voice sobbed.

"I love you very much. I just don't want you to hurt our

children again," Allan said.

"Allan, I still love you too," Anna said. "I want to be your wife again. I miss you and the other kids."

"I've already given you enough chances. There's a pattern, it's repeated enough, and it's hurt us enough. If you wanted to stay my wife, you wouldn't have tried to leave."

"I didn't want to leave," Anna protested.

"No, Anna, you did," Allan said. "You've gone back and forth saying you love me and you hate me and the kids. I don't know what to believe anymore. That doesn't make for a healthy family."

Anna's sobs gradated to anger.

"I knew you were cheating on me. But with who? Are you still seeing her? I know you are, right now! Is that why you wouldn't let me back home, because she was there? Whatever, please just send me some money if you can?"

Allan shook his head, trusting it was Anna's pain talking. He didn't have the time or energy to waste, however. And he was growing irritable. "Ok, look," he said. "I'll send you ten-thousand once if that's what you want. Use it well and take care of the twins. Please."

Anna's voice calmed again. "Ok...thank you. I love you Allan."

Already under pressure, Allan snapped. "That doesn't mean anything anymore."

He hung up promptly, before he might say anything else.

\*\*\*

94

Anna got the money Allan sent.

But she wasn't going to stop there. There was an immense void in her spirit and she wanted to fill it. If Allan wouldn't fill it with acceptance, she would get it through what he owned. She decided to take him to court for selling the house without her approval.

Anna was intent of getting a hold of everything Allan had– or as much as she could.

That Monday before she got her court hearing, Allan called her and told her she needed to go to the bank and see how much more money he put in for her and the boys. Allan had deposited one million dollars.

She called Allan back promptly.

"Allan? Why did you put in so much?"

"They paid me three million dollars for the house," Allan replied. "You get one, million, kept another million for myself, and I've left another million for all eight of our children as their inheritance."

"Thank, you Allan," she said. "I love you."

Allan groaned audibly over the phone. "This isn't love, Anna. Going between saying you love me, hate me, even our kids. A moment ago you were trying to sue me for everything when I'm keeping healthy boundaries. Now you go back to saying you love me because I made you happy. Anna, love is a commitment. When people love each other they are loyal to eachother. They don't flip-flop. I don't know what to believe from you anymore. Just be smart with that money for your sake and the sake of the twins. We don't have anything else to talk about. Honestly, for everything you put me and the kids through, I shouldn't owe you shit. Good-bye."

"Wait! Allan!" Anna said, "Where are you living now? At least just tell me that."

"Closer to the kids, who are in college. Bye, Anna."

Allan hung up.

Anna's emotions exploded and she slammed her phone down. How was she going to keep an eye on her family if she didn't know where they were anymore? Allan knew where she was living.

"Ronnie?" Anna called. "I have a job for you. I'll give you a thousand dollars."

***

Alex and the others were putting the house back together before they started school.

Andy would be starting Pre-Kindergarten this year, but he wasn't looking forward to it. "Can I go to school with Alex, Dad?" he asked.

"No, you have to go to your school first," Allan tried to encourage him.

On Andy's first day of school, he cried when his father left. Allan stayed around for a few minutes more until Andy's teacher got him playing outside. Allan left after that so he wouldn't be late for work. Andy cried again when he saw his father was gone. His teacher wasn't able to control him, so she said, "Andy what about your mom do you want me to call her and have her come pick you

96

up?"

Andy sobbed, "My mom doesn't live with me anymore."

His teacher called Allan at work, but he was in a meeting. He returned her call, however, saying he would be there I'll be there as soon as he could.

By the time he got there, Andy was playing with another little boy.

"Wow, what happened?" Allan asked.

Andy's teacher said, "That little boy's name is Alex. When Alex told all of us his name, your son said, 'My big brother's name is Alex too!' From that moment on they have been together."

When Andy saw his father, he ran over and gave him a hug. "Dad, gues what. My best friend's name is Alex just like my brother. How cool is that?"

Alex's mother arrived shortly thereafter, since Pre-K was drawing to a close, and the boy, Alex, ran to tell about his new best friend, Andy.

"That's my best friend's Mommy." Andy said.

"You wanna go say hi?" Allan asked.

Both parents walked over and met each other, exchanging cordial introductions.

Andy and Alex said good-bye after that, but both were ecstatic to see each other against tomorrow.

***

Andy talked for the rest of that day about his new school. He called his big brother Alex later that day, and was eager to tell him about his new best friend by the same name.

"There are a lot of boys named Alex," Andy's big brother laughed.

"Well," Andy replied, "I have the best. Because one Alex's is my big brother, and the other is my best friend."

"Well, I'm happy for you, little buddy." Alex said. "Can I talk to dad? Is he there?"

Andy gave the phone to Allan.

"Hey Alex," Allan said.

"Hey, Dad," Alex sighed, his demanor changing to defeat. "Amy left me again. I'm starting my new job tomorrow at the law office, and she does this to me again!"

Allan sighed, "Boy. Has she been around your mother to learn how to do this shit?"

"Well, are Amanda or Mark there? I'm wondering if one or both would be willing to come to my house. I need some help."

"They're both here," Allan said. "I'll ask them. I'm sorry about all this, son."

"I just really appreciate everything, Dad."

Amanda and Mark left to help Alex shortly after their call.

***

Allan needed a nanny to live at the house and help with the younger kids, cook, clean, and be able to take them to school and pick them up. He tasked Amanda to help him look.

After two days of searching, Amanda had four candidates whom she met with. The first two opted out of the job when they heard more details. The third candidate was all right, and for a while, Amanda considered hiring her, though she was very new and had other responsibilities.

The final candidate was thirty minutes late, but humbly apologized and explained he got lost. After his interview, Amanda more interested in hiring him. His name was Chris. He was thirty-seven years old. He wasn't able to have children, nor did he ever marry, but Amanda could see he had what it took to be the nanny the family needed. So she asked him to come back to the house and meet every one else to see what they thought of him. She suspected all would like him, though Andy might be more shy than most.

Right after the interview, Amanda allowed Chris to come into the family's house and meet Allan first. "He's the best man for this job," Amanda vouched. "Besides, a male will be better for Andy, and I'm sure the other girls will like him too."

The girls came down and met Chris, and they seemed to get along well with him just as Amanda thought they would. When Andy ran into the house he stopped and looked at his father. "Who is this? Who is this man?"

Allan picked up his son in his arms. "This is Chris. He's going to move in and help take care of you, and the house, and he'll be cooking for all of us."

Andy didn't say anything, and seemed apprehensive.

"Go play, now so Chris and I can talk about everything, ok?" he let Andy down and Andy did so.

Chris smiled humbly. "So you have decided to select me then, sir?" he asked.

"Yes," Allan replied. "First off, is two-thousand a month

not enough money?"

"That's more than enough money, thank you sir," Chris replied.

"Wonderful. So as Amanda explained, I'm sure, you will need to take the kids to and from school, keep the house clean and cook dinner on Monday through Thursday, and Friday nights we will do take out. You have weekends off unless I will need you situationally for the weekends. I will try to ask three days beforehand, but or it could be minute's notice as well. I'll pay you extra any time you need to work on the weekend."

"Thank you. I can start. This Monday, but I'll can in the day before: Sunday after church. Is that all right with you sir?"

"That's perfect," Allan said.

No sooner had he spoke, Alyssa and Amber could be heard fighting upstairs again.

Allan groaned. "I've had it with those girls. Just a moment, Chris."

"Allan," Chris said. "May I, sir? You can see me at work."

"Go for it, Chris."

Chris went to the stairs and called both the girls to go and stand in the corner.

"Think about why I put you here. Now go!"

Both Alyssa and Amber did as they were told from Chris. Afterward, Chris asked them to come and stand in front of him. "Tell me why I put you there."

Both girls said, "Because we were fighting again."

"Girls, the next time you both fight will get one-hundred

minutes to stand there for fighting. Do we understand?"

Both said, "Yes sir."

Chris and Allan reconvened downstairs.

"That was amazing, Chris. How did you learn to do that stuff? College?"

Chris replied, "I did go to college to learn to handle children. I love children. Just can't have my own. So I dedicated my life helping other parents raise theirs."

Andy came over to Chris and asked him all kinds of questions, and Chris answered them all in truth and Andy.

Alex came up to the house to meet Chris. Everybody seem to really like Chris. So on Sunday, Chris moved in his new room and into his part of the house.

"I can help you with your stuff if you need me to," Chris offered to Andy.

By Friday, Andy loved Chris so much he was his sidekick now.

***

Meanwhile, Anna was busy with the twins getting them ready for their weekend at the fun park for kids.

Ronnie returned that day, with information on where Allan with living.

Anna had paid Ronnie a lot of money for follow Allan's children from school, conspicuously, and find out where they were living. She looked up the phone number for the address in public records and called Allan, while she now paid Ronnie a lot of money to take care of the twins.

Allan did not return Anna's call. That just made Anna more angry. By the end of the week, Anna was so mad at him that she let out her emotions on Allan badly in her voicemail.

By that moment, Allan was having enough of Anna not respecting his boundaries. He saw now she was stalking him somehow, and had found the phone number to the house. He called her back and when she answered the phone.

"Shut up and listen!" Allan said. "Look, I don't want to hear your voice. I don't care if you die tomorrow. I wouldn't cry over you. Plus you hurting our children the way that you did several times, is enough! I don't believe you when you say you love me, because you flipflop, you're not sincere. You need to stay away, like you wanted! You've had your life with us, I offered you grace, you blew it time and time again. Now go to Hell! Don't ever call me again!"

Allan hung up the phone, and cried privately.

He never wanted to have to say all of that to her, he knew those words were very hurtful, but she needed to hear them so she would go away.

Anna called him back one more time, but only to confirm, she would never call him again.

\*\*\*

Alex was working nights and going to school during the day.

Amanda was on her second year of college. She wanted to be a teacher. Alyssa would start college in two more years, and then Amber would start college four years afterward. Allison would start in six years, then would be little Andy, who just started Pre-K.

Allan wanted to spend each of those twelve years of children as preciously as he could, and see each of them off with a good life. The family had seen so much turbulence already, he could only hope to help his children build the best future they could have out of this.

***

Andy and his best friend Alex were together every day at school. The two boys were always together. Their families also allowed they to say over at Andy's house for the weekend—Chris was permitted to pick up both kids from school.

On the way home, somebody almost hit the back end of the car by running a red light! When Allan got home, Chris notified Allan. Allan suggested going another way home to be safer, though Chris was certain it was a mishap and the road wasn't any more or less dangerous.

Andy meanwhile was upstairs sharing his room with his best friend Alex.

Allan called all his kids downstairs to see what they wanted for dinner for takeout.

Everyone wanted pizza.

"Daddy can we have ice cream after dinner? Please?" asked Andy.

"Yes, we can," Allan said. "Chris, will you go to the store for me?"

"Please get ice cream, cherries, chocolate and strawberry syrup, and bananas for the kids. Vanilla and chocolate chip ice cream please."

"Gallon's of each?" Chris asked.

"Yes, thank you so very much. I'll get the pizza in about an hour."

That night, they all had so much fun with Alan and Chris for his first week as the home Nanny. Chris had become a big part of the family. Allan made everyone banana splits and put a lot of cherries on top for the boys. They rented three movies, and while eating their ice cream they were watching the first Movie. Allen put the two boys to bed. He told the girls they could stay up as long as they don't fight. So they didn't fight that night.

Saturday afternoon, however, Amber and Allison were hitting each other and yelling.

Chris went upstairs and forcefully separated each one of them.

"Now go downstairs. I'll be right there," Chris told them.

They left, and Chris asked, Alyssa—who had also been present—if she saw who started the fight. Alyssa said Allison started it this time.

Chris walked downstairs, and the girls were waiting for him. "Amber, you can go stand in the corner," he said. "Allison you may come with me. Write one-hundred times on this piece of paper, 'I will not start any more fights.' Then tonight, after dinner, you will do the dishes and the cleanup with me. Do you understand me?"

Allison wrote as Chris said. It took her about an hour to do so.

Amber was already back in her room.

Allan was surprised to find Chris was disciplining the girls on Saturday.

"Chris, you are off on weekends," Allan reassured him.

"I know, sir, but these girls have to learn to stop fighting over stupid stuff, regardless. I just hope that this works well. I have used this before with my other children, it usually words after the second time. It teached them to keep their word. If I believe in anything, its that children from a young age should know to keep their word, work well, and be the best they can be."

Little Andy pitched in and said to everybody, "I will always keep my word to anybody I say. I'll always do my best at whatever I do."

"That's good, my son," Allan said. "I'm very proud of you, Andy."

***

The following Mondya, Andy got his first report card from pre-k. H was getting so smart. He loved learning how to read and write.

"Dad after dinner can I read you a book? So you can hear me read a book?"

Allan said, "Yes, of course! You can read all of us a book if you like."

"Oh, yeah!" Andy said.

After dinner and the cleanup was done everybody came into the living room. Andy got into his father's lap and read, *The Little Red Hen,* based on the classic folktale. Chris and his brother Alex listened especially. Andy only missed one word in the story. His father looked at his son, saying, "You can read that really good, son!"

"Daddy, I'm always reading books! I really want to go buy some new books, Daddy. I have read almost all my books in my room. The girls won't let me see or use their books. They say I'm too young to read those books."

***

Allan complimetned Andy's teacher the next moring on his way to work, after Chris dropped him off.

"All Andy loves doing is reading," the teacher said. "At story time, I have to let him read two times a week if not he starts to cry. He can read at second grade level right now. I want to have him tested before school. He may be able to go straight to the first grade!"

When Andy heard what they were talking about, however, he walked over to them both.

"No! I'm not leaving my best friend Alex back in this grade. If he can't go, then I don't go."

His teacher looked at Andy and said, "You know Alex is going with you, right?"

"Really?" Allan asked. "Alex too?"

The teacher responded, "The two of them just read and read together. You should be very proud of your son."

Allan grinned and said, "Well, let's put him in kindergarten and see how he does. Growing up is more than just academics, it's social and behavioral too."

The teacher nodded. "That's what Alex's mother said to do. Regardless, I bet the boys go so far in school. I could see them finishing high school when they're sixteen years old! Be able to go to college, but too young to start!"

Allan was beaming. "I could only hope so."

Though he knew the future was full of surprises—many of them unwelcome.

# Chapter 7

Anna was getting ready for work on a Monday morning.

She left the twins with Ronnie, kissed them and told them how much she loved them, before walking out the door into her car and drove off.

She was passing through an intersection when a big truck hit her car by the driver's side door by someone running from the cops. Her car spun clockwise several times until it came to a full stop. Anna lost focus, perceiving smoke, fire, and broken glass, the interior drenched in blood. She could hear sirens surrounding her.

She kept lapsing in and out of consciousness...Anna saw her life flash before her eyes, all her greatest memories, all her greatest sorrows and regrets, all her hopes and dreams, all her worries for the future of her family: Allan and each child.

She felt she was before fought over before hope and despair.

When she awoke again, the EMTs were getting her out of the car. Anna heard overheard them saying they weren't sure she would make it.

Anna already knew.

She passed into the hospital doors. All she could think of was how sorry she was for any failures and what would become of each of her family. Would her efforts to repair any damage have been enough? Would they remember every good lesson she hoped to instill in them?

Would they be okay?

Anna closed her eyes, knowing it would be the last time. She was so afraid of what she had left behind, terrified it was a mess. A disaster.

Darkness surrounded her. Her senses shut down a final time as she wallowed in a sense of sorrowful doom that threatened to snatch her.

But the last thing she registered while she still breathed her last, was not a sense terror or sorrow or despair. One final sense of calm washed over her, and the darkness that flooded and surrounded her was not that a destructive torment, but a peaceful repose.

She felt like she was a baby being held in a mother's embrace, safe and protected and comforted. All she could hear was what sounded like her own voice repeating words of comfort and protection, and power and strength, for herself and for her family.

"I will always love you."

***

Allan was at work when he got a call from the hospital in

Idaho—which immediately alarmed him. He worried the twins might be sick again.

"Hello? This is Allan."

"Hello sir, I'm one of the nurses here who cared for your twins."

"Are they all right?" Allan asked.

"Sir, your wife, Anna was hit by a drunk driver this morning."

Allan felt color leave his face. He heard the nurse continuing to speak, but he couldn't register what else she was saying. He went into a crazed internal shut down. Afterward, he ran out of his office straight for his car.

He called Chris, and when he answered, he yelled and withheld frightful sobs, "Chris! Please don't say anything to the other kids. If they ask where I am, you say I had to go out of town for a day or so, please Chris! I'll call you when I know more."

***

Allan made it to the hospital that same day and went straight to the nurse's unit and asked for his wife. They told him where she was, and Allan hurried straight up to her room, yelling, "Anna! Anna!"

The doctor stopped Allan right before he got to her room and said sternly, but calmly. "Sir, I'll be with you shortly."

Allan went to the waiting room, breaking down alone for a moment.

The doctor came in, and Allan ran up to him, but before he could ask, the doctor looked at Allan in the eyes. He didn't need to

110

say anything. Allan knew.

He was still standing, but felt he could collapse in a heap on the spot.

"We did all we could, Allan," the doctor said.

He walked Allan into the room where they put her. Anna's lifeless body was disfigured almost beyond recognition.

"Would you like to say your goodbyes to her?" the doctor asked.

All Allan could do was nod slowly as shock held his sense captive. The doctor left him alone.

Allan recalled the last words he had told Anna when she was alive. He wished he could take them back even they seemed necessary at the time. Now it didn't matter. He just wanted to tell Anna how much he still loved her, and have her hear it and listen. He wanted to hear her response, see her smile, and exchange one last sign of peace between himself and her.

Now it was too late.

Now he had everything back, including the twins who would also come home now, all at the precious cost of forfeiting Anna.

It hurt. It hurt everywhere. Not a single thread of Allan's being knew any peace or wellness.

***

Allan drove by Anna's house to see them playing in the yard under watch of Ronnie. He got out of the car, and to his surprise, the boys knew who he was, calling him, "Daddy."

Ronnie seemed to recognize him as well. "You're Allan," he

said. "I'm Ronnie, I'm the boy's nanny. Is everything all right?"

Allan knew Ronnie could see he must looked stricken.

"Ronnie, can we meet inside the house please? I have something to tell you about Anna."

Ronnie called the boy inside and Allan sat down with Ronnie in the living room.

"Anna was killed today on her way to work," Allan explained. "A drunk driver killed her. I heard the guy who hit her was not even hurt."

\*\*\*

Allan had to buy two car seats for the boys. Later that night, he returned home to Chris would was keeping watch on the rest of the family. Amanda came running outside to her father concernedly. Allan gave her a hug and asked her for her help getting the twins into the house. Afterward, Allan told Amanda to call Alex and Allison.

Amanda, called them both, saying, "Dad needs us. Right now! He's here with the twins, get over her, please. *Right now!*"

When all eight children were seated down, Allan braced himself to give the news to them all.

"Today on your mother's way to work, a man ran a red light and hit your mother's door. He was drinking and driving. Your mother was killed. The doctors did all they could for her. She passed five hours after she was hit. That's why we now have the twins back."

\*\*\*

Alex and Chris drove to Idaho the next day went down to

his mother's house to get the twin's things. Ronnie was still there keeping the house in good shape. Alex recognized the house was setup just like Anna, his mother, used to have everything–the subtle ways she laid everything out.

He went into his mother's room and sat down on her bed a short moment before the agony he'd been holding in overtook him. He buried his head into his hands and started crying like a baby.

Chris heard him crying and went to the room and sat down next to Alex.

"Hey," he said. "I'll be right there if you want to have somebody to talk to about anything. I've lost my mother too. I know what this is like. I've been here before."

Alex cried bitterly and only nodded. When he could hold himself together again, he stood up and said, "Let's get this done."

Alex started packing his mother's room with Chris. Ronnie also offered to help, but Alex told Ronnie to leave everything else. The only things he wanted were pictures of all the kids.

*** 

Alex that night stayed in his mother's room. Her bed felt so soft. He could catch his mother's fragrance on it. He fell asleep in minutes and when he woke up he cried his eyes out all over the next day.

That same day Ronnie left the house, and Chris and Alex returned home.

Allan was standing in the driveway, waiting. When they pulled into the driveway, as soon as the car had stopped, Alex jumped out of the truck and ran over to his father and started to cry in his father's arms.

All Allan could do was hold his son close to him.

Amanda and the other girls came outside later. Amanda opened the back door to the truck. When the started going through their mother's stuff, many started crying.

The only one who did not know who his mother was was Andy.

Andy started asking everybody why they were sad and when they asked him if he remembered who Mom was, Andy said, "No."

Allison couldn't take it any more and went to her room crying. She didn't come out for the rest of the day–she was still too angry at her mother that she didn't want to hear anything nice about her.

***

That night when everybody went to sleep, Amanda knocked on their father's door and came into the room. Her father was sitting in his chair. She sat down on the bed and in looked up at her dad and started crying, and saying to him she was so mad at her mother still, but she was also hurt by her death. She admitted she didn't want to be around during the funeral service. She did not have the capacity.

On the day they laid Anna to rest, Amanda was not present. She didn't want anything to do with it. She was sitting in her room when the family came home from putting their mother to rest. They found her crying hard.

Allan went into her room sat next to her and held her as close as he could to him, while the others gathered around.

"I know, Amanda, how you hurt," he said. "I hurt just as much as you kids do. That lady was the love of my life."

As Amanda cried into her father's shoulder, Chris came in too.

"I do understand what you all are going through," he added. "My parents died when I was twenty-one years old. They were killed at my home when I was hiding in my closet under some bags. They didn't find me in the house."

Alex looked at Chris. "Who didn't find you?" he asked.

Chris said, "An intruder. I went out of the house into the living room after they left and saw both my parents shot." Chris's eyes gazed at the floor as he showed his vulnerability with the family. "I wish I still had my parents. But kids...even if you just have your father left spend all the time who can with him. I'll be here for you all too. I truly hope that this will be over soon but you need to understand that God can turn any ugly tragedy into something better. Someday you may all see."

"Chris?" Allan said. "Do you think we could get you to go get some subs and chips and soda and pizzas for everybody?"

"Yes sir," said Chris.

Little Andy spoke up then, "Can I go with you chris?"

Allan nodded, "You may, if Chris says you can."

Chris smiled again and said, "Let's go little buddy."

***

After the family had taken the time they needed to mourn,

115

Amanda and Mark made an announcement during dinner one night.

They both stood up and Amanda said, "Everybody, we have something to say to you. Mark and I are going to have a baby! I'm ten weeks, and doing great! We are all very happy about it!"

Allan then got up from the table, but he did not look pleased. "You want kids after all the shit your mother put you kids through? Then she dies and leaves me to pick up and raise everyone of you and I don't know how!"

Amanda and Mark regarded each other with some regret for the timing of the announcement. They hadn't realized Allan would still be withholding some distress.

Feeling out of place, still, was little Andy. He looked at everybody and said, "I don't know who mom is? I want to know her so bad."

Andy had only seen pictures of Anna. He was only three years old when she had been taken. He was very upset that he didn't know her like the others.

***

The following day, Alex spent a long afternoon looking out the window in a trance. He wished he could have seen his mother one more time. He knew his relationship with his mother had been turbulent. He thought that day at the hospital in Idaho, he'd rightly torn into her. Now those last mean things he remembered saying to her didn't feel so justified. Now there were no more chances.

Alex's phone rang. It was his old girlfriend Amy. Against

116

Alex's better judgement, he answered.

Amy told him she was having his baby.

Alex replied telling her he would wait to see a DNA test to see if the baby really was his. Amy also told him she intended to tell his father.

After the call, Alex told Chris the news. Chris thought it was wise not to tell Allan for now—given he was still emotionally compromised. He advised to wait until Alex knew the baby was his.

Alex said wondered how they would keep Allan from hearing about it, since Amy said she was going to speak up. Chris could only hope that Amy didn't get to speak a word.

Unfortunately, Amy reached Allan by phone that same day.

Chris went into Allan's office, having overheard the conversation, to let Allan know Alex was waiting for a DNA test.

All Allan could do was throw his arm up.

"The hell Is going on with my children?" he groaned. "I can't keep buying new houses for everybody here! All because my family keeps growing bigger!"

To Chris's pleasant surprise, Allan smiled afterward. It was genuinely happy.

"Alex!" Allan said. "Come into my office!"

When Alex walked in, Allan ran at him with open arms yelling, "I'm going to be a grandpa two times now! I love it son! Now you and Amy gotta get married to raise your children together!"

Alex backed away, alarmed, saying, "But Dad, what if the

baby isn't mine? I don't want to raise somebody else's kids. I don't want to if I don't have to."

"At least be open to the possibility," Allan told him. "Besides, even if you're not the father, what if the other guy isn't so great? Every child deserves a good father and I know you'd make a noble one. At least be opened to giving the baby a loving home, if there isn't anyone else who can."

Alex trembled. "I'll think about it, Dad. It's gonna be hard."

Allan set his hands on his son's arm. "I just wish your mother was here to enjoy being a grandma."

"I know she is here with us," Alex said, withholding sobs.

Allan looked into his son's eyes.

"I just wish I could tell her I'm sorry. Now I can't. But you were right Dad. There was humanity in her. Maybe we had those boundaries, then, but regardless, she loved us. And we all loved her. There's no hiding from that. She loved us to her death, I know it. Now she won't ever go anywhere," Alex continued. "She will be right here with us until then. And I hope someday that you have a hundred grandchildren and they all live here with you."

Allan scoffed with a smile. "Not a hundred, I hope! I'd be in over my head."

"You and mom had *us* all together. You don't think all of us are not going to have kids too? In your dreams dad!"

At this point, Chris let Allan and Alex be. When people talked about kids, he became emotional.

***

Alyssa and Allison were fighting again. There quarrel could

118

be heard across the house.

Chris opened the door to Allan's office,

"We got another fight going on," he said.

"I hear it," Allan got up promptly, hearing the sounds of physical battery.

They both ran upstairs. Allan grabbed Alyssa and Chris restrained Allison. Even when pulled apart, they were trying to fight each other.

"Alyssa, stop!" Allan told his daughter.

"She started it, this time, Dad!" Allison shouted. "I didn't start this one!"

"Really, Allison?" Chris asked doubtfully. "You always start them."

"Well, she's wearing my shirt and she didn't ask me at all!" Alyssa yelled. "So I told her to take it off, and Allison said make me so I was making her take it off!"

Chris groaned. "Both of you girls know better than to fight over stuff like this. This makes it six times this week. So give me your cell phones. Both of you are grounded. But this time, you two are grounded from your rooms or having anybody come over for the summer. And you will be doing a summer job, at *my* office. Do you both understand me this time!?"

"Chris!" Alyssa cried.

"That's insane!" sobbed Allison.

*"That's* insane? No. Your fighting *is*, honestly," Chris said. "And if you girls fight within this summer, time will be added on. Understand?"

Both girls surrendered with a "Yes sir."

Chris headed back to the living room. Allan followed after him, sighing with relief.

"I love the way you handle the fights," Allan congratulated.

"Every time it's different, but this year it's bound to get them to stop. I should hope," Chris said. "Plus after a summer working for me, they don't know want to know what will happen next time."

***

Ten days after that fight, the girls asked their father privately if they could have their room back. Allan was scarcely about to object when he received a call on his phone.

"I need to talk to Allan," the voice on the other line asked.

"This is him," Allan said.

"You have a daughter named Amanda, and Son in law named Mark, yes?"

"Yes," Allan answered.

"We need you to come down to the nurses's station so we can talk."

Alan's felt like he was choking. All he could think about was the awful possibilities of what could be happening this time. "I'll be right there. Thank you."

Allan called for Chris and told him to watch the house until he got back.

***

Allan was seated in the waiting room promptly when he arrived at the hospital. The doctor came into to the waiting room

120

then. Allan stood up and went over to him. "Please," he said. "Whatever happened, please tell me she is not dead."

The doctor answered, "No. But she did lose the baby. Both Amanda and Mark are in the ICU. We're not sure yet if she will wake up. Mark is doing better than she is, he not longer needs to be in a unit, we just really want to watch him tonight. He wants to be next to Amanda."

Allan was already pieces, and now he felt ready to come unbound.

"I'll take you to her now," the doctor said. "Please sir, be strong for your daughter."

The doctor helped Allan as he tread weakly into the ICU. He saw his daughter lying in an the intensive care unit. Mark was sitting beside her, crying bitterly over her.

"Please, God don't let her die, please," Mark sobbed. "Don't take her from me, I want to love her still!"

Allan almost started to cry himself, but held it back. He went over and took Mark into his arm. "It's all going to be all right, Mark," he said as Mark leaned into Allan. He felt like he didn't have any strength to sit up. "Come on," Allan said. "Let's lay you down and you get you some rest, yourself."

***

Chris listened over the phone as Allan told him what he knew.

"Do you want me to tell you the others? So they know what is going on?" Chris asked.

"No," Allan replied. "I just want you to tell Alex to to come here, and I'll meet him in the ICU waiting room. I'll have him here so I can come home and tell the kids."

"Yes sir," Chris said.

***

Alex showed up at the Hospital soon as Chris gave him the message.

He met his father in the ICU waiting room.

"What happened?" Alex asked.

"Seems they were attacked," Allan said. "We don't know who or why."

Alex's jaw dropped.

"Mark is awake, but he isn't saying much, yet." Allan said. "Go sit here until I get back. If anything happens you are to call me, ok? I have to go and let the other kids know."

***

Allan walked into the house. All kids were sitting in the living room waiting on their father. Allan didn't have to breathe a word, because the rest of his family had caught the news on television. They saw footage of Mark standing over Amanda in the Hospital."

"Dad how is she?" Amber asked.

It took all the strength Allan had to hold himself together, and it didn't feel enough to last long.

"Well, you guys," Allan sighed, "I can't say is she holding her own. Because she is not. She is still asleep and the doctor doesn't know if she will ever wake up again. Mark is all right, they are just watching him overnight."

122

Allan sat down as he felt his chest getting heavy, burying his face in his hands. "Whoever did this, I gonna kill them."

Chris sat beside Allan as his children surrounded him.

"Both Mark and Amanda," Allan wept. "The doctors really don't know if she'll wake up. And she lost the baby!"

Chris was scarcely about to comfort Allan, when Alex called.

Allan picked up. "Son?" he asked.

"Dad, you need to get over here now," Alex said. His tone of voice grave. "And...I'm not sure if I should call the cops."

"What the hell do you mean?" Allan asked.

"Amanda woke up, and she tried yelling something. She even tried taking the breathing tube out of her mouth to tell me, and now she can't wake up again."

"What did she try to tell you?!"

*** 

When Allan got back to the Hospital he walked into the ICU and went over to Amanda's bed with Alex. "Amanda," Allan said. "Did Mark try to kill you? Move your right hand if Mark tried to kill you."

Amanda's right hand twitched with urgent intent, with what little strength she had left.

"My daughter," Allan said.

Allan strode over went over to Mark's bed, hands hands making fists.

"Mark you need to get up," he growled. "You are going to tell me the truth!"

Mark woke up and looked Allan in the eye with alarm.

The doctor looked at Allan and intervened. "Sir," he said.

"Son of bitch!" Allan hissed as he prepared to throw fists. The Doctor sternly to restrain Allan.

Two cops arrived promptly, stepping into the ICU.

Mark looked at Alex ragefully. "The bitch had it coming to her," he said. "Amanda was a whore and the baby was not my baby. They did a DNA test and it said the baby is *not mine!*"

"So you tried to kill her because she was cheating on you?" Alex yelled.

"That's right," Mark said to Alex face coldly.

"You're dead!" Alex shouted as he charged for Mark.

He was restrained by the cops promptly.

"I heard you two fighting!" Alex yelled in a feral tone. "Two or three times, but if I knew you were this low, I'd have sent you to hell myself in a heartbeat!"

"I called you my son!" Allan joined, both men ready to kill.

Both police officers restrained Alex and Allan and called for backup.

At that moment, alarms rang for Amanda's vitals.

"Amanda!" Alex shouted.

Amanda, no!" Allan cried.

Mark stood up and actively intervened with the medical staff, upluging her unit as much as he could deliberately. "She deserves it!" he said. "She won't get away with cheating on me! Having another man's baby and trying to pass it off as *my baby!* Oh she's gonna burn! She's burning in hell now, real good!"

The ICU room was in pandemonium. Both Alex and Allan saw red from Mark's taunts, until backup arrived from law enforcement to secure the scene.

***

Allan was pacing the floor of the hospital waiting room. His mind was holding in a wild craze and fear. It took all his energy and then some to contain it.

Alex was sitting in a chair and trembling in place. A two police officers kept guard with them..

Mark had been detained—he was outside in a police car in handcuffs.

The doctor walked into the waiting room, sighing.

"I'm so sorry," he said. "We did everything we could for her."

Allan shut down on his feet, unable to speak any word of reply.

"Even if she had lived she'd never walked again or had children. But we tried regardless."

Allan's mind only played memories. So many memories. He also remembered that little Andy was Amanda's son, but nobody knew. Now Andy would never know Amanda as his mother.

Allan collapsed in a chair and cried. He cried so hard his hurt excruciatingly.

Alex was gritting his teeth and breaking down, also in terrible paid. He hugged his father, wishing to be there for him.

Allan went outside, followed by a police officer and saw

Mark handcuffed in the back of the police vehicle. He was crying as well. Allan heard him praying as he walked up, "I didn't mean to do all that. Please God don't take her from me!"

Allan looked at Mark with a killing gaze with police watched on guard. "You're are going to jail, tonight, big guy," Allan boomed. "For killing my daughter. You sorry son of a bitch."

Allan turned and stormed off, hearing Mark begin to scream behind him. He held no remorse—he would let Mark feel sorry. Allan also knew if he stayed with him, he could get out of control again.

He never wanted to see Mark again.

Alex met Allan at the hospital doors.

"Dad, there is a man in the waiting room wanting to see you."

Allan walked into the waiting room. There was a very tall man standing there.

"Hello sir. Allan?" he said, reaching out his hand. "I'm Andrew. I was wondering how Amanda was doing?"

Allan shook, but his handshake was weak and defeated. "How do you know, Amanda?"

"I'm her boyfriend, sir," Andrew said. "Yes, I know about that son of a bitch, Mark. Now, at least. Amanda never told me she was seeing anyone else. I just wish she had, I didn't think it was like her. How bad is she hurt? What about Mark?"

Allan's eyes were glazed over on the floor. "They just took Mark to jail for killing Amanda," he replied.

"My gosh," Andrew said. "I'm so, sir," Andrew flopped in a

chair and shook his head in disbelief, shutting down as well. "If only I'd known the truth," was all he could say. "If only I just knew the truth."

***

When Allan walked into the house everyone was asleep but Chris. Chris looked up at Allan, and at once, he knew.

They walked into Allan's office. And Allan proceeded to tell Chris everything that unfolded.

As they did so, Andrew walked in. Chris looked up and said, "Who is this?"

Allan regarded Andrew briefly. "His name is Andrew. Amanda had been cheating on Mark with him. Andrew never knew. I've invited him a stay a while."

Andrew sat in a third chair and. "I just wish she'd have told me," he burred his face in his hands. "For sixteen months. All of this over hiding a relationship with another man."

He began to openly recall everything in front of Allan and Chris. The other girls had woken up and were gathering at the door too.

"We were just friends at first. We were coworkers at her job. One day we went to lunch together, and I saw it looked like someone had hit her in the face. I know now that it was Mark, but she told me she'd bumped in the door." He paused. "I...I started to get suspicious when I saw she had other marks on her back and arms and legs." He started to cry. "I should have asked what was going on. I should've spoken up then." He took a while to compose himself. "A week later Amanda came into work and I saw she'd been crying. I asked her what was happening, she said it was fine, but I knew it wasn't. After work I met her privately and asked if someone was hurting her. That I'd seen the marks on her back, legs, arms, the night we made love. She told me was fine and she just drove off in a hurry, but I knew then someone was hurting Amanda. I just didn't know who. We met some nights later at my home, I tried to comfort her and it escalated into us making love again. I saw the beating was worse...the next morning I asked her why would wouldn't say anything. She told me because I would have killed 'him.' I Thought maybe she meant a father or another family member, I didn't know she was seeing another man. Until this morning...I learned Mark had hit Amanda several times like crazy this morning in a driveway and then he ran her over with his own car, before he started hurting himself. He'd even smashed his face in the window."

Allison started crying really hard. "Amanda," she sobbed, caving in on herself spiritually. "I'll never get to borrow her shoes again," she said.

"No shit Allison," Alyssa sobbed angrily. "She's dead, just like our mother. Now we never get to meet her baby."

Andrew looked up at the two girls before he looked at Allan. "Sir? May I speak to them?"

Allan nodded.

Andrew looked at Allan's daughters. "Alyssa right?" he asked.

"Yes, and why should you care?"

"How do you know her name?" Allison asked.

"Well," Andrew replied, "First off, I care because I know what you are feeling right now. I really, really loved Amanda too. I also know that Allan is not your real father."

"How?"

"Your sister told me," Andrew siad. "Alyssa, almost three years ago I lost my only brother in an accident. He lived for three days and then I went to go see him after school at the hospital. My brother died in my arms. I was never so lost, until I lost my only brother. My parents only had my brother and myself. All the time we have together...it's special. It's precious. You never know when it will end and be taken away. For now, just remember all the good times you had with Amanda. That can never be taken away. And Amanda will always live on in your hearts. As she will mine."

Alyssa looked at the ground somberly before looking up at Andrew. "Thank you," she siad. "Why would Mark do that to my sister? Beat her up and try to kill her and the baby?"

"I don't know the answer to your question," Andrew said. "Maybe in court some answers will come up. I'm just sorry...I'm so, so sorry."

Allan had been quiet for a long time, but looked up. "Chris? You know where Alex is?"

"No, sir," Chris said. "His truck is outside, but I haven't seen him."

Allan braced himself and got up. "Okay, I'm going to walk over to the back house and see if he is there, and if he needs anything?"

***

Allan knocked on the door to the backhouse. No one answered, so he let himself in. Alex was sitting in his sister's room, crying.

"Why couldn't I know?" Alex asked. "Why couldn't I know Mark was beating her?! I should have known something! I'm so sorry, Amanda. Why didn't you tell me? Now God has my mother and my sister!"

Allan touched his son's shoulder.

Alex looked up and his father was crying as well. They sat together holding each other and crying together. They were joined by the rest of the family minutes later. Before long all the family was present in Amanda's room.

Even little Andy.

The family had taken time to compose themselves, Alyssa spoke up.

"What's going to happen to Amanda's stuff?" She picked up the shoes from her sister she loved dearly and held them to her chest. "Dad?" she sobbed. "Could I please have her shoes and the Vernal? I'll take good care fo them for Amanda."

Allan shed another tear and smiled. "Yes you may."

Alyssa cried again and hugged her father.

"We'll pick out a casket and make sure they will put her to rest next to Mother."

"Dad?" asked Allison. "What about the baby? Did she know what they were going to name the baby?"

"I don't know...but maybe Andrew can choose a name, if he hasn't already. We can ask him."

Allan squeezed Alyssa into his arm extra. "Alyssa," he said. "You're the second oldest child now. The oldest girl I have I now. What that comes a lot more responsibility, more than you may be used to. But you'll learn in time. Alyssa, there should be no more fighting with your sisters. You are now the new role model."

Alyssa forced a smile. "Yes sir," she said. "I'll be the best sister I can be."

***

Alyssa spent the next afternoon picking out every little thing that she knew her sister would love. She picked Amanda's favorite dress that she loved so much, the same that their mother bought it for Amanda. As she going through everything, she a moment to sit on Amanda's bed to cry. Alex sat beside her, crying as well.

"I don't know what to do," Alyssa said. "I miss Amanda, and now I have to be the new role model. I'm afraid I won't be good enough."

Alex wrapped his arm around his sister's shoulder. "And I'm wondering how I can be so strong through this?" Alex asked. "I know I have to because of our father. But I feel like I'm gonna crumble. I'm not strong. Growing up in our family, I never knew any of this was going to happen to us. I don't know what's next."

***

Many people went to the viewing during Amanda's funeral service.

Alyssa had spent much time before hand making sure everything was in his place and everything was done right for her

131

sister. When they laid Amanda to rest at her grave site, there were more than six-hundred surrounding. Even some of her high school friends and teachers had come.

Amanda's family had no idea how many lives she had touched. They knew she had done much for her friends and for others during her time on earth—more than she ever let anyone know about.

***

Mark's trial proceeded some days later. Evidence was collected to convict him—not only the witnesses who gave testimony to having see him uplug her ICU at the hospital and intervene with medical staff, but evidence was collected from Amanda's phone, as well as Allan's voicemail.

She had tried to call the night, Mark had run her over.

"Only if you are dead you whore!" Mark's voice shouted in the background of the message she had left.

"I love you, family," Amanda said. "I love you, family."

Andrew was crying, just as Allan, and Chris as well.

Allan was silently furious, even just being in the same place as Mark. The man he trusted to take care of his daughter, the man he once called a son.

***

After the trial had adjourned and Mark was sentenced, Allan and Alex found Andrew leaning on the wall alone outside the court building.

In the months that had followed, Andrew had become family, even through ironic circumstances.

"I really miss my friend so much," Andrew sighed.

"I know, you do," Alex said compassionately.

"It's gonna be hard going home," Andrew said, reflecting. "The whole office at work feels so different without Amanda too. Truth be told I'm looking to move out too. I need to find a new place to stay."

Allan took a moment to think.

"Are you now?" he asked. "Well, we have that back house over there. My son lives there by himself now."

Andrew's eyes lit up, in shock. "You're offering me a home?" he asked. "With you guys?"

Alex grinned when he heard the idea. "Hell yeah. If that's all right with you, Andrew?"

Andrew's eyes moistened, "Yes that's great."

Little Andy walked up, having overheard the conversation. "Andrew?" he asked.

Andrew looked down, "Yep. That's me."

Andy smirked, "I think you have *my* name, sir," he joked.

The men laughed together.

Andy went on, "I hope you like living over here with all of us, but the girls fight alot. Chris takes very good care of us tho. Are you going to move in with my brother?"

"That's right," Andrew said.

"Cool," said Andy. "Now you will have us all to you. Amanda took very good care of us too."

Andrew nodded. "I know she did. She always spoke of you all highly."

"Oh, and one more thing," Andy said. "You are not Big Andy, because you are Andrew. And I'm a Little Andy. That's what Amanda called me."

Andrew smiled. "Deal."

***

Weeks past, and the weeks turned into months. Much to everyone's delight, the girls hadn't fought at all during that time. The twin boys, however could be found punching each other. Whenever Chris told them to stop, they would say, "We're just playing around, we are not the girls."

Just the same, Alyssa was acting more grown up than before. Everyone seemed to like the way she had changed.

Sometimes they mistook her for Amanda, herself. They saw a lot of Amanda in her.

# Chapter 8

On Friday when Allan came home from work he called all the family and told them all to go get dressed up. They were all going out to dinner. Even Chris and Andrew.

All three girls dressed their nicest. Little Andy and Andrew were wearing the same colors—neither of them knew until they saw each other. Allison and Amber helped to get the twin boys dressed up—the twins would be entering pre-kindergarten next month.

A limo arrived to pick up the family. The twin boys had never been in a limo before and were excited to try it. Andrew told them it was his first time as well. Amber asked her dad what the special occasion was for. Allan told her they were meeting someone tonight, but he kept it a surprise. All he asked was that everyone was on their best behavior.

The driver of the limo pulled up into the restaurant of Allan's choice, and the family got out. When they walked into the restaurant, Amber heard her father ask the waiter if, 'Elizabeth' was there yet.

As he asked speaking, a woman walked in through the

entrance, "She's right behind you, Allan," the woman said.

Allan looked back at the woman and smiled.

"Elizabeth," he said, "Meet my children: Alex, Alyssa, Amber, Allison, Andy, Anthony, and Adam. These other two men are Andrew and Chris. They're family too."

He then put his arm around. "Everyone, Elizabeth and I have been dating for almost one year. I thought it was time for you all to meet each other."

Everyone was shocked. Not even Chris had known about this.

Alex was the first one to speak up. "You kept quiet all this time about this?" he asked.

Allan answered him, "I thought it was important to take it slow and carefully. Especially for your sakes."

The family was on their best behavior throughout the evening, but there was an uneasy tension at the table.

"Well kids you all are going home with Chris tonight on the limo," Allan told them. "I'll see you guys tomorrow."

Allison spoke up. "Dad, I don't like her at all. Can you just to come home with all of us?"

"Stop Allison," Alyssa spoke up. "You're not being very nice."

Alyssa looked over at her Father and proceeded, "So I guess you are going home with her, dad?"

"Yes, I am, tomorrow morning," said Allan. "Be good kids for Chris please. I hope this is all right with you, Chris?"

"Of course, sir, it is. I love being around them."

On their way back to the limo, Alyssa spoke up, trying to ease the tension.

"Dad is happy," she said. "He's given all of us his life. He deserves to be happy!"

***

Allan got more than ten calls from Allison that night. Allan let them all go to voice mail.

"Allison really doesn't like this," he groaned.

Elizabeth regarded his mood understandingly. "All I can say is that the little one wants her daddy to be at home with them. It's been like that her whole life."

"And my twin boys are starting school this coming fall," Allan said. "There's gonna be some huge changes at home."

"Allan," Elizabeth said. "I have something I would love to know. About Anna."

Allan looked up at her.

Elizabeth went on, saying, "If she wanted all of those kids, why did she leave them all with you but the twin boys?"

Allan sighed. "I've had my suspicions," he said. "The twins are going to be five years old and they are going to need shots for school. When they do, I want their DNA tested."

"When will that be?"

"Either this mongth or August," Allan said. "Then I'll know if they are mine or...someone elses."

Elizabeth asked, "and what if they're not yours?"

Allan chuckled. "I'll cross that bridge when we come to it. But I love them as my own no matter what."

137

*** 

Little Andy just loved Andrew. In the months that passed they had gotten close. Every time Andy greeted him he said, "What's up, Little me?"

Andrew would grin and say, "Hey, you are the little one not me."

The summer that went by, Elizabeth got to be more acquainted with Allan's family, traveling to waterparks, theme parks, and having so much fun. Allison even came around to like her afterall. The family was growing.

Amy and Alex got married right after Alex found out her child was his. They would be having a daughter.

Alex and Chris kept her at home so that Alex could finish his last year of college. In addition, Alex was working part-time.

The baby's name was Alice.

The day after their last trip to a theme park for the summer, the twin boys went to the doctor's for their shots. Allan had also scheduled a DNA test. The doctor said he would have the results in fifteen days or less.

Fourteen days later, the doctor called Allan.

"You need to come down and meet me after work."

***

Allan walked into the doctor's office promptly after he clocked out. She had him sit down and get comfortable.

"Allan," the doctor said, "There is a 99.9% those are, indeed, your sons. But we have something else to talk about."

"What is it?" Allan asked.

"It's Adam. I need to run some more tests on him," she answered. "His blood work shows there is a chance of cancer somewhere in his body."

Allan sinking weight in his core.

"We may have a long road ahead of all of us, the doctor siad."

***

Allan brought Adam back to the clinic the next day in the morning for those test. Chris called when he had a private moment.

"Why did Adam have to go back to the doctor?" Chris asked.

"He might have cancer," Allan told him. "The doctor is hoping that the cancer isn't in his blood directly, at least. They're runnning some more tests right now."

Allan's son, Adam, was giving a room they made just for him—he would be their all day. The doctor wanted to rule the first test out. After it was completed, the Doctor walked in and sighed.

"Allan," she said. "Your son has a very bad form of blood cancer called leukemia. We are going to have to put him in the hospital."

Allan collapsed in a heap where he sat, shaking his head in unbelief.

"Now here's another bump in the road for our family," he moaned.

***

After the drive home, Adam ran into the house, into his

room, and slammed his door.

Allan felt the stares from every single person once he stepped into the house as well.

He told them the news.

"He may not want to play or be around everybody," he explained. "I'm sorry to have to tell you kids more bad news. But let's hope that the doctor found it in time for it to go away."

Andrew approached.

"Allan, may I please try and talk to him?" he asked.

"Yes you can try," Allan replied. "Anybody can try. Just go easy on him."

Andrew knocked on the door.

"Go away!" Adam yelled.

"It's Andrew. Can I please just have a moment?"

Adam opened the door, albeit unhappily.

Andrew walked inside and asked if he could sit down.

"I want to tell you a little story about a boy your age," Andrew said. "He had the same thing you do and now he lives with your family." Andrew pointed to himself. "And that family loves him a lot. Adam, cancer is just a word the doctors use to make us worry over nothing. But if you start now by doing anything you can to make time much better. Like, I'll start working out with you every morning, if you like. Anything to make this easier for you. I'll be right here by your side."

"You had cancer, Andrew?" Adam asked.

"Yes and I still do," Andrew said. "It's just sleeping right now. But I make the most of my life every day, because my life is

140

precious. So is yours."

***

Andrew was talking to Adam, Little Andy approached Chris.

"We really need to talk," Andry said.

Chris looked at Andy, with concern. "Did something happen today at school?" he asked.

"There is this bully. He pushes me around me, shoves himself into me all rude, and he won't stop. And if I tell on him, the third graders will not like me."

"Well little, Andy," Chris said. "Tonight after dinner, you meet me in my room. I'll teach you to stand your ground."

For the remainder of the day, Andy kept talking to his sisters about how Chris is going to teach him how to punch.

The next day at school, Andy was met with his bully as usual. He walked right up to Andy and pushed him down. Andy got back up after three times of being pushed to the ground, repeatedly telling the bully to stop and warned him if he tried again he would defend himself.

The bully laughed and came up to Andy for another push. Andy gave him a right punch in the face, then followed up with a left and another right. The bully went down to the ground, shocked and a crowd of other students began to gather at the commotion.

"Now leave me alone!" Andy said. "Or I'll be *your* bully, and you won't like it! Got it?!"

Consequently, Andy was told to go to the principal's office

when his teacher witnessed the display. But when Andy got home he walked with a new kind of confidence. Chris and Allan could see it in his stride.

"Sorry that I didn't come to you, Dad, about my bully, but I can't always walk away. You got to face your bullies! And Chris, I want to thank you! I kicked his ass today at school! I warned him like you said and when he didn't listen, I just gave him a right punch and followed up with a one-two! Then I told him he better leave me alone!"

Chris smirked. "I like your new confidence, Andy! Remember, don't let it get to your head. You're not a bully like the other guy, but a good kid."

"Maybe you'll be a boxer," Allan added. "The next million-dollar man."

Chris smiled. "That's only if he wants to," he said.

"I do!" Andy said. "Can you teach me, Chris?"

"All right then," Chris said. "I'll take you to a boxing ring and see what you think about it."

***

Adam's doctor called the next day, and told Allan to come down to the hospital as soon as possible and to bring Adam with him.

They both left for the doctor's office. Adam was not feeling that good today. He didn't say anything to anybody. As soon as the nurse looked at Adam, she picked him up and put him in a hospital room. Fifteen minutes later, the doctor came in and told Allan to sit down. Adam was put into the hospital for stagecancern.

\*\*\*

Andy was now going by, "Little Andy Slugger," from Chris and he loved it.

That night after dinner, Andy and Chris went to the boxing ring. The minute they walked in, Little Andy Slugger loved everything he saw. Especially the punching bag.

"Slugger, you must really like that punching bag," Chris said, seeing how Andy took to it. His punches and hacks showed promise. "Do you know how to jump rope?" Chris asked.

"Jump rope?" Andy said quizzically. "That's for girls!"

Chris laughed. "Slugger, guys who box love to jump rope! It's part of their job. Maybe next time I show you. Your father and Adam should be home by now. Come on."

"Ok," Andy said. "But I want to come back here! I'm going to like it!"

"Then I'll take you every night if you like."

\*\*\*

Allan arrived and informed the family that Adam would still be at the Hospital. He might be there as long as six-weeks.

"Can I tell you kids something?" Allan said. "Everything that has happened to our family has been done for a reason. Maybe not everything that happened was right, but even if it wasn't, God allowed it, because bad things that happen can be turned around for good, somehow. Maybe sometimes it's hard to see or believe it, but it you wait patiently and keep looking for the right signs, you can see and understand. Right, now, it's ok if it's

143

hard to understand. I'm with you. When I die, I have so many questions for God. That's how I feel right now."

"How is Adam handling the Hospital by himself?" Chris asked.

"He's not alone," Allan answered. "Elizabeth is there with him. I'll tell you something Chris, he loves Elizabeth. He told me today. He told me to go home and shower, get clean clothes on, and then come back here."

Alex, Allison, and Amber all went to see their baby brother in the Hospital when Allan returned. When Alex and the girls went into his room. Adam was in Elizabeth's arms, asleep like a baby. Alex went up to her and asked quietly, "Can I hold my baby brother?"

"Yes," Elizabeth said. *"If* you think you can pick him up, he is really heavy."

Alex picked up Adam, who opened his eyes. When he saw Alex, Adam started to cry and reached out for Elizabeth again. So Alex gave Adam back.

"He's been doing that with your father, too," Elizabeth explained. "He doesn't want anybody holding him but me. So that's what I am have been doing. Just sitting here holding this little baby."

Allison and Amber came in from the gift shop with many presents.

Adam's eyes lit right up. "Are those all for me?" he asked.

They had balloons, and even a teddy bear that was bigger than Adam himself. He loved that teddy bear. He went over to his sisters and said thank you! I love you guys so much!"

Then he went back to Elizabeth and she picked him up. "I'm going to sleep now. I'll see you guys tomorrow."

Alex heard Adam call Elizabeth, "Mommy." Nothing was sweeter that day for Alex.

***

Allan was still home when the kids got there.

Alex walked over to his father.

"When did Adam start calling Elizabeth, 'Mommy?'"

"What?" Allan asked. "You heard him call her that?"

"Yeah."

"Well," Allan said, flashing a smile. "I didn't know he was, but that's great. He did that all on his own."

***

Chris, Andrew, Anthony, and Andy were going to play cards at home. All four were sitting at the table, playing war with the cards, when Allison came in from yelling at somebody outside.

Chris looked at her and said, "What was that all about?"

"None of your business, that's what!" Allusion replied.

Chris stood up and walked over to the door and opened it.

"Well if it's none of my business then get out and don't bring stuff that is none of my business in this house. What's going on outside?"

"I don't have to tell you," Allison said. "It's none of your business!"

"Then go to your room. It's for talking to me the way you are, now go."

145

Allison, told Chris, "Go to Hell!"

"Really?" Chris asked, unphased. "You're going to talk to me like *that* now? Go to your room now allison."

"And I told you to go to Hell, Chris!" Allison shouted.

Alex walked in through the back door and heard what Allison said to Chris. "Young lady, you need to watch your mouth for one, and two, do as Chris told you to do now. Three, why are there like six people in front in our yard?"

"None of your business, Alex!" Allison growled furiously.

Chris said, "If there are six people on our front yard, it's our business now."

Stepping outside, there were six kids and six sets of parents waiting. The parents all started yelling at Allison and Chris about how Allison is being a bully on the street.

"She has been saying nasty things to out kids on this street and now she's been hitting and pushing all of them down and stealing their bikes and hiding them all over the place!"

"We are still missing two of the bikes!"

Chris looked at Allison and said, "Go get those two bikes now! Then go to the house and sit there at the table and wait for me to come in there."

When Allison left, begrudgingly, Chris started talking to the parents and told them that none of this will ever happen again because she will be grounded for a week. After one week, she will be coming over to each their houses and she will be doing something kind for each one of the children she bullied.

When Allison returned with the bikes, Chris met her inside

the house–he caught her occupying his own room.

"Allison get out of my room," Chris said. "I asked you to wait at the table for me. I hope you understand that you are grounded for one week. And after that week, every day for the next twelve days afterward, you are going spend two days at each house doing something nice for each kid you that you bullied. Now me your cell phone."

"Wait until you see my father!" Allison shouted. "He will fire you!"

"Allison, go call your-" Chris began, "No never mind. *I'll* call him. Right now."

Chris called Allan, but Allan replied, "Chris, I'll call you right back," and hung up.

Chris looked at Allison and said, "I wonder what's going on. And if it's your brother."

Thirty minutes later, Allan called Chris back. "Hey," Allan said, sounding upset. "I'll...I'll see you guys in twenty minutes," and hung up again.

When Allan got home everyone was waiting for him. He entered the room and sat down in his chair, bracing himself.

"Adam is going to die very soon," Allan said. "So tomorrow, your brother is coming home with a bed and machines. I need help from all of you, because I want his bed inside my room. The one they are bringing to us. Then I'm going to buy one and put it downstairs so he can  see everybody and play if he wants to."

"No, Dad," Alex walked up, eyes moist. "No, Adam won't die if he comes home! He's gotta get better. He really misses

Anthony and Anthony is missing Adam so much, he keeps saying I want to play. He keeps saying that my brother and I need him."

Alex broke down, and Allan embraced his son.

***

Allan went back to the Hospital with Alex and Adam's twin, Anthony. The nurses and hospital staff kept telling them, "You never told us he has a twin brother. Maybe that's why he doesn't want to do anything not even eat."

Alex carried Adam out to the hallway. When Adam and Anthony saw each other, Adam got down from Alex's arms and run to his twin brother. They collided into each other's arms and hugged tight.

Once home, Adam walked back into his room. Anthony and Adam got into the bed and started talking. They talked to the point where only they knew what they were saying to each other.

"Wow," Elizabeth said, watching fondly from outside the room with Alex. "That's why he wanted me to hold him all the time. He missed his twin. He missed his family. Just family."

"Yes," Alex said, containing himself by a thread. "Hospital staff can be kind, and friendly, but kids need their family."

"Everyone needs their family." Elizabeth said.

Meanwhile, Allison strode straight up to her father and said, "Daddy you must fire Chris! Right now, Daddy!"

"Why Allison?" Allan groaned.

"Because he grounded me for no reason at all!"

Allan sighed. He didn't have time for this.

"Just go get Chris and ask him to come here, and meet me

148

in my office, please," he said.

Allison proudly stalked to Chris's room.

"My daddy wants you in his office to fire you!" she spat.

"Quite," Chris sighed, nonchalantly.

Chris walked to Allan's office, knocked, and was let in.

Allan sat in his seat, exhausted and troubled. "What is going on with Allison?"

Chris sat down in a chair opposite from Allan. "It's a long story, we'll be here for a while."

"Give me the short story of it all," Allan said.

Chris nodded, understandingly. "Allison will be in here as well. She is being the block bully. Hitting, pushing, stealing bikes and hiding them all over the place. We had six sets of parents here last night yelling at her, all while Allison tried telling me it's, 'None of my business,' and to, 'Go to hell.'"

"Allison? Being a bully?" Allan fell back in his chair. "She's been so sweet though?"

"She went from sweet to sour," Chris said, shaking his head.

Allison walked into the office, folding her arms as though expecting to watch her victory unfold. Instead, Allan looked her in the eye, and called her by all three of her names. "Get your ass in his chair now!"

"Let alone," Chris said, "When I asked her to meet me at the dining room table, I caught her in my room. So I grounded her for a week and at the end, for twelve days, she will spend time with the kids she was being a bully too, doing nice things for

149

them. From morning until afternoon."

***

Alex stayed near Adam and Anthony, watching them playing together happily. Allan walked into the room. "You're free to head home Alex," he said. "I need you to help Chris with Allison. Anthony is staying the night with Adam here."

Alex hugged bother Adam and Anthony tightly. "See you guys at home tomorrow," he said.

On cue, Allison's voice began yelling insults and curses at Chris, one after another. Her voice could be heard in every room in the house, perhaps even into the neighbor's walls.

Alex arrived where Allison was verbally assaulting Chris and grabbed his sister by the arm.

"Who and the fuck do you think you are yelling at Chris that way. Go to your room and one of us will call you when dinner is done. Then you can go to the dinner table and sit there until bedtime or whatever Chris tells you. You will do as Chris tells you, until you learn to grow up. Do you understand me? Allison!?"

"Mind your own business, Alex!"

Alex glared at his sister. "We all live under this roof, this *is* my business. This is all of our business. So you better watch your mouth or I'll smack it for you."

"And you need to watch *your* mouth or else smack it for *you*. Then I'll tell Daddy on you. You will be in so much trouble, Alex!"

"Oh yeah," Alex said. "Like the way he fired Chris. Good job, Allison."

150

Chris said, "I'm calling your dad now. And I'm putting him on speaker."

He did just that, and Allan picked up.

"Hello, Chris what's up?"

"Sir, it's Allison," Chris said. "She is just being very rude and disrespectful to myself and Alex, telling us to mind our own business."

"Chris would you put your phone in Allison's hand or put it on speaker phone so I may talk to her?"

"You are on speaker, sir," said Chris.

"Young lady," Allan said. "You need to go to your room and stay there tonight. Do you understand me?"

Allison replied, "Yes sir, I understand you, daddy."

"I truly would watch your mouth for the rest of the night," Allan proceeded.

"Okay Daddy. I love you."

"Now." Allan said.

Allison went to her room and slammed her door.

***

The following morning, Allison woke to the sound of drills in her doorway.

She sat up to see Chris with the drills, unhinging it.

"Chris!" Allison yelled. "Give me my door back! Give me my door back now, Chris, you sorry son of a bitch! Now my daddy will fire you this time! I know it."

Looked held Allison's door in his arm and began to carry it off. "Allison, please go and sit at the table."

"Fine!" Allison barked. "But you better give my door back first!"

"Go now, young lady." Chris siad.

Allison stomped her feet all the way there, and sat down the stairs and sat in a chair at the dining room table. She started to cry and kept on crying until her dad walked into the dining room.

"Daddy!" Allison said. "Chris is being mean to me again! Fire him! Please!"

Allan stopped her and called her by her three names again. "Get your ass into to my office! Now!"

Allison went to her father's office, and when he walked in, he said, "Allison you are going to summer boot camp."

"Why are you sending me away to that place?!" Allison exclaimed, shocked.

"Look everything you have done and still are doing," Allan said. "You're being a bully on the neighborhood, taking out your rage on Chris, disobeying and disrespecting everyone in this house, including me! All while your younger brother is dying. I don't have time for this abuse from you right now, so in two days you are leaving to go to boot camp school."

***

Two days later, Allan got Allison ready, and they left the house before noon.

When Allison saw the school building outside the car window, she began to plead, "Dad, please don't make me do this! Daddy, I'll be good, I promise Daddy! I'll be good, Daddy. I promise you so much!"

"You already had that chance. You already had those warnings. You've earned this," Allan reprimanded.

Allison broke down in tears. "I just don't know what to do!" she sobbed. "Mother died, and then Amanda died on me. Now Adam!"

"I really wish your mother was here for you too," Allan said, sternly. "But your behavior is making things a lot worse. Not better. Not for us, and especially not for you."

"So what dad!" she sobbed. "I was going to go to mom's house that weekend that she was killed!"

"What?" Allan asked. "Without telling me?"

"Do you understand how you guys felt about me not letting here come back home?! That broke my heart! I missed my mom everyday since she left! But at the same time I hate her for leaving me alone!"

Allan could only sigh as he kept driving.

"Dad, why do I have to go to boot camp?! I don't want to go Daddy! I promise I'll be a good girl daddy! I'll stop being a bully! Never again, Daddy."

"No Allison," Allan said parking the car. "I want you to go here for 2 weeks. Those are the consequences for your actions. After that, *if* you are still not liking it, I'll come and get you. And you will behave maturely and kindly when you come home then."

Allison spoke through her sobs. "Ok," she said. "I'll go here for two weeks. I know I won't like it, but I'll see you in two weeks. Will you'll be here this fast, Daddy?"

"Yes," Allan said, speaking with as much comfort as he could afford. "I'll be here this fast. Herecomes your teacher."

Allison and Allan saw the instructor walking toward the car.

"I know I would have to fight with you," Allan said. "Plus I don't have the heart. Allison, I know how bad it was for all you kids. I never felt so bad for you kids, after everything the family has been through. I want the best for you all, and I clearly don't have what it takes at this stage to see you grow up into a mature, healthy, happy, responsible adult right now. This is why I'm making this decision."

"All right, Dad," Allison said, not looking up and rying her tears. "I'll see you in two weeks," She opened the car door, grinding her teeth bitterly. "Just tell Chris I said, 'Thank you for making me go to boot camp school!' It's all his fault and he knows it's too!"

"I don't think so Allison," Allan said. "It has always been your choice, everything you did. It's to come here to boot camp."

"Well, *I* don't think so Dad! It's *his* fault and he knows it is!"

Allison's instructor walked up behind her, arms folded. "You must be Allison."

"Yes," Allison replied. "I am Allison."

"Good. Now tell you Father goodbye and come here with me please so we can get your stuff out of the the trunk and carry it up the stairs to your room. I'll help you move in. All your things must be put away in 1 hour and your bed will be made and everything has to be in place. So put everything away. I'll see you in 1 hour from now."

"Yes, ma'am," Allison said. "Thank you."

# Chapter 9

Both of Adam's beds were dropped off later that afternoon as Allan was driving home. He put one in his room and the other in the living room–wherever Adam wanted to sleep at any time. Every morning, the nurse was there to help, and by noon, another nurse was there to assist. Finally a third nurse helped him until evening.

Despite whatever the nurses did for him, Adam continued to get sicker.

"There are foods out there that can help him with his kind of cancer," Amber said to Allan privately one day. "So why don't people just go and learn a little bit about them. What is wrong with them? When I'm a doctor, I am going to make sure that I always have something for the people I see and read about it first."

Allan turned to her proudly.

"I want to be a doctor, Dad," she said. "When I grow up."

"An admirable profession," Allan said. "What kind of

doctor do you want to be?"

"I want to work children who have cancer," Amber answered. "Not just because Adam. I think of all those kids with cancer and how sick they looked. I want to help. For now, we take Adam to see his twin, Anthony, and see now happy that makes them both. Being twins, they share one thing that nobody but twins share. Just think, they same bond for nine months in the womb too. That company, that love for each other before their born."

Allan listed to Amber with a full heart—she spoke with words of life—life he'd been needing to hear a long time.

"Well Dad, it's good talking to you," Amber said, "But I'm going to go and read now. I'll see you later."

"All right," Allan replied. "Would you ask Chris and Andrew to come here for me please."

"Sure."

***

Both Chris and Andrew walked into Allan's office.

"Boys," Allan said. "I got a dang good idea. That is if you are up for it. It'll take the both of you to do this. In about three weeks, I'm going to start working from home. Three days a week. Maybe four, and then just work at office during the remainder of weekdays. I'll need one of you to take the morning shift with Adam, and the other the afternoon shift, with his nurses. Then I'll be home in the evening to help with the last shift. So what I need is for you guys to help the twins with their school for now until I can find somebody to come in and be a homeschool teacher for

them. I don't want the boys to be apart like that ever again while
they grow up. The time they have which each other is precious."

A knock came at his door.

"Come in," Allan said.

It was Amber. "Can I help with the boys two?"

Allan smiled, his heart full all over again. "All right,
Amber," he said. "You are hired as tutor number three, until I find
someone.

Alex walked into house from downstairs.

"Allison?" Alex asked.

"Excuse me," Allan said.

He walked downstair to meet Alex.

"Allison's already gone to bootcamp," he said. "I truly hate
having to send her there, and that she is gone and not here with
us. With Adam let alone. I just couldn't handle her anymore. Chris
has been at his wits end too. I just don't understand how she
could do the things she has been doing or why. Well...I suppose I
know why. But I don't know why *now?* She was such a sweet girl,
she's never been like this before."

***

Allison called her father that evening, crying to him.

"Daddy, I don't want to stay here!" Allison sobbed. "This is
all your fault!"

"Who's fault is is going to be next?" Allan sighed. "It's
everyone's fault but your own with you, isn't it. Why is it all my
fault?"

The phone hung up.

Amber meanwhile tutored her twin brothers with devotion. She insisted she help with morning and afternoon shifts, and then some. She even wanted to sleep on the chair next to her brother's bed, which ever bed her took. She wanted to be close to him always. She was savoring every moment. Allan and Chris and Andrew even agreed to put one of the bed in Amber's room, if she wanted, and Amber agreed happily.

"I'd like the bed here please," Amber said, motioning to the spot she liked. "I want his bed right here. I'll do everything else for my brother. I love him so much and nobody will ever take that away from me. No one will ever take *him* away from me."

At that moment, Adam came in, holding his head, crying. Amber picked him up and held him. "Hey, Adam, what happened?"

"Little Andy hit me in the head with the ball!" Adam sobbed. "My head hurts!"

Amber consoled him. "Well he didn't mean to hit you. It was an accident. I'm sure Andy feels bad, besides."

"Amber, where is Mommy Elizabeth? I want her."

Allan kissed Adam on the head. "I'll come get her now," he said.

Elizabeth came right over soon after and picked up crying Adam. And said, "It's okay baby it's all right. I got you now."

Adam rested his head on Elizabeth's should. "I missed Mommy," he moaned.

Elizabeth just held him next to her until he fell asleep. She laid him down in his bed—which was now in Amber's own room.

Anthony went to his bed, and the next morning, the twins awoke side by side together in Adam's bed.

Alex awoke that morning to help out with the twins for their moring schooling. Amber was already awake and waiting on the nurse—who was nearly twenty minutes late today. Amber put it in her new book of records. Amber even confronted the nurse about it that evening. The nurse, to say the least was impressed how Amber was an aspiring physician. "Next time you should call the doctor so we can write it down in *our* books we are keeping on Adam."

That evening, after schooling and treatment, Adam didn't even want to play. He went back to sleep. The next morning, Adam was simply exhausted. When Alex came back from school he met with Adam in Amber's room and could tell it was more than Adam feeling sick—he was emotionally fatigued.

"Hey, what's up Adam?" Alex asked.

Adam looked at Alex sadly.

Alex smiled. "Champ we are not going to lay in this bed all day. Come on, how about we go to the zoo later. Would you like that?"

Adam flash a little smile and nodded.

"We'll go after the nurses give you that stuff."

"How can you call it 'stuff?'" Adam said disgustedly. "Between you mean, I feel like it's making me sicker."

"I know buddy," Alex said. "Just one three more weeks of it and then you'll be done for a month."

"Then we start again after that." Adam groaned.

"I know. But it will only be two hours a day, then."

\*\*\*

Anthony, Adam, and Alex all went to the zoo after Adam's second treatment. They took Alex's daughter, little Alice, with them. They enjoyed the trip to the fullest of their capacity, and were home thirty minutes before Adam he had to endure the third treatment that day.

Adam asked Elizabeth if, after his treatment was done, he could visit Alex and Amy, and get to hold Alice and feed her a bottle. Alex told him, yes, he could.

When they arrived at Alex's house, Amy was not please.

"I don't want him over here," she said. "He is sick and he could give it to Alice. I don't want him close to our baby at all."

Alex glared. "How dare you not let Adam get close to Alice. He's not contagious! And you are not being very nice."

\*\*\*

Later that night, Adam overheard Alex talking to his father. Amy wanted to break up with him. Again.

She didn't even want Alice.

"I'm just so done with this," Alex said. "At this rate, I've given her more than enough chances. I'm grown up, and I think she's still stuck in a high schooler's mindset. I guess I'll let her go."

"Well," Adam said. "That's fine with all of us. Because Alice is your baby, right brother?"

Alex smiled. How could he be so upset now with Adam's wisdom. "Yes," Alex said. "She is my baby. And she'll have a good home."

Adam smiled and went to play in the room with his twin, Anthony.

Amber walked in as they were having fun and asked them, "Are you boys wanting dinner now? Let's eat some lunch before it gets any later. And it is already late."

That evening at the dinner table, Allan told everybody that after Adam had his last treatment in the evening tomorrow, they were all going to Mark's Baked Pizza Barn. There they had video games, rides, golf, and everyone could eat pizza, ice cream, cake, and pie.

"All for my kids," he said. "Kids of all ages! This is where Adam wants to go, so that's right where we all are going to do. I'm also going to pick up Allison for this this afternoon. She'll be going back to bootcamp the tomorrow in the morning."

"All of us are going to Mark's Baked Pizza barn!" Adam asked with a radiant grin.

"Oh boy, we will have so much fun there, kids!" Allan said.

"And is Elizabeth going too, Daddy?" asked Amber.

Allan frowned. "No," he said. "We are not seeing each other anymore."

A heart breaking silence collapsed over the dining room.

"Why not?" asked Amber.

"She went right back to her old boyfriend again."

Amber winced.

Allan winced back, to indicate he'd explain more later in private.

That evening, Allan revealed more to Amber alone. He was

sure to be very delicate.

"Elizabeth's boyfriend got out of jail," he said. "He was imprisoned for beating her. Elizabeth told me how he almost killed her."

"But she went right back to *him?*" Amber asked, her face struck with disgust as much as shock. "Why would she do that?"

Allan bowed his head. "I've seen this a lot as a lawyer," he explained. "More than I'd like. Human beings get attached to each other easily. Sometimes, the bond is toxic, but many still choose that toxic bond over a real warm, healthy one. I wish more people out there knew that bonds and attachment are not the same thing as love. But unfortunately, not everyone knows the difference. And when they don't, people get hurt," Allan spoke sadly. "People suffer. Even our family has seen our share of that."

Amber could only bow her head and ponder quietly.

***

Allan picked up allison from bootcamp in the morning. They were home by that afternoon. The relief and the and exhaustion and the safety was written all over Allison's face. First thing she did was run right up to Chris and hugged him.

"I'm sorry," she said, beginning to sob. "It will never happen again. None of it."

When Alex saw her, she ran up to him crying, sobs becoming full crying, and gave him a turn with a hug. "I'm sorry brother, forgive me, please brother."

Alex held Allison tenderly. "We are always going to be all right in the end, sister."

Alex went into his room and greeted Adam. "Hey little buddy," he said.

Adam was laughing so hard at something.

Alex looked around. "Where's Anthony?"

Anthony jumped out of the big dresser drawer and shouted! Alex grabbed his chest and screamed in fright from the surprise. Adam's suppressed giggles became hysterical laughter. Allan and Chris ran into the boys room asking what going on, and found all three of them laughing.

"Who screamed?" Allan asked.

Adam tried to say, "Alex" but was laughing too hard.

"I did that," said Alex. "Another jumped out of the dresser and I nearly soiled by pants."

"That sounded like a girl's scream, too," Chris taunted.

Adam's laughter erupted he might have pulled a muscle.

***

Allison even got to hold Alice that day.

"She's gotten so big!" Allison said. "I've only been gone for, what? Two months? Boy look at her. Alex where is Amy, is she working?"

Alex groaned. "Hell, no. When Adam came home she wouldn't let Adam get close to her or Alice. I told her off about it and...she wanted to leave. Everyone. So I let her have what she wanted. But my daughter is not going anywhere."

"Amy just left?" Allison asked. "Even Alice?"

"Almost pushed us down," Alex said. "She ran out so fast and said she was going to go and find a rich doctor or lawyer or

164

something. No phone calls or any sign or word from her since. Ever since Adam came home."

Allan walked and put his biggest smile on.

"Well everybody we have one more hour before we leave to Mark's Big Pizza Barn. Who's happy right now?"

"I am, Daddy!" Adam shouted.

***

Three o'clock in the afternoon, everybody got into one van and Allan started driving.

When he got to the freeway traffic nearly halted them to a stop.

"Can see you what is going on up there?" Amber asked.

Allan winced his eyes. "Yes," he said. "There's some woman running from the cops and...oh dear." He said under his breath, "she's naked."

"Lovely," Allison groaned.

Alex, who was sitting up front winced his own eyes. "Wait," he said.

He opened the door.

"Alex?" Allan asked.

"I'll be right back," Alex told his father.

Alex ran up toward the commotion. "Amy?!" Alex called out.

One of the cops approached Alex, "Sir, do you know this woman?"

"I do," Alex said. "Her name is Amy. She's...well, we're legally married, but still."

"Can you see if see if she will come to you please? We have been doing this too long."

Alex called her name three times, and then she looked at him, and ran over to him.

"Alex!" she said. "I'm doing this all for you, Alex! I love you!"

"Okay, can you come here? So I can put my coat around you, please Amy."

"All right!" Amy run up to him.

Alex grabbed her arm, but was dismissed by the police, who proceeded to put her on the ground and handcuff her.

The police told Alex, "Thank you."

An applause erupted from down the street from drivers waiting to move forward.

Alex sighed in relief and walked back toward the van as he was bombarded with praise the whole way.

When he got back inside the van, Allan eyed him.

"Was that?" Allan began to ask.

"Yep," Alex answered. "It was."

***

Allan proceed driving. When he took the exit nearest to their destination, he spoke up again. "When we get there I'm going to go in first, alone. So that I can make sure everything is done right for Adam. They're setting the place up special, just for him."

They pulled into the parking lot and Allan got out. "Be right back."

The family watched him walk into the building.

Fifteen minutes later, he came walking back to the car. "Hold on," he said, "There's one thing that's just for Adam and Anthony. Everyone else stay right here."

Allan helped Adam and Anthony out of the van. "Go on kids," he said.

Allan, Adam, and Anthony walked into Mark's Big Pizza Barn. The twin's eyes got so big when they saw how big it is inside.

All these people jumped out of places you would have never guessed they'd been hiding, each saying, "The twins rock!"

Adam and Anthony looked at each other and started speaking to each other what felt like their secret language– babbling of cheer and joy.

The rest of the family joined with them afterward, and the celebration began. Pizza, ice cream, candy, video games, and rides too.

The twins wanted Andy, Andrew, Alex, and Chris to go on a ride with them. They were joined on the ride with the girls as well. The only one screaming was Allison. When they got off the ride Allison went to her dad crying because the ride scared her senseless.

Allison and her father went back to the table and sat down. All Allison wanted to talk about was school–she was enjoying it!

Chris joined at the table later and sat next to her. "I hear you really it over there at Bootcamp?" he said.

"Yes sir," said Allison. "I really love it. I want to stay there until I go to college!"

Chris smirked and said, "Is it still my fault you're there?"

"Hell, yes it is your fault," she said.

Chris looked at Allison and snickered. "Well I'm sorry you feel that way, because I had something for you. I'll it when we get home later."

***

When the festivities had run their course, Allan and Chris started gathering the kids, telling them it was time to go home.

No one knew, however, where Adam and Anthony were.

Chris took it on himself to find them while Allan gather there rest. He sensed something was wrong.

Chris found Anthony sitting next to Adam behind several arcade machines, alone. Anthony was crying. Adam was lying on the floor, still and pale.

"Allan! Chris shouted. "Call 911! Now!"

Allan told Andrew to call on his behalf and met Chris at the scene. Andrew joined later, communicating with the dispatcher over cell phone.

Chris was checking Adam's vitals.

"Is he still breathing?" Allan asked.

"Yes but very little. He's only sipping air."

Paramedics rushed inside Mark's Pizza Barn and took over with Adam.

"Alex," Allan told his son, "Come with us. Sit with Anthony where he can see Adam."

Adam stopped breathing by the time the ambulance made it to the hospital. He was taken into the ER. Only Allan was admitted inside.

They were losing Adam. They called code blue. Every doctor and nurse went running inside. The head nurse looked at Allan and told him, "Can you please go to the waiting room until the doctor comes to talk to you."

Allan felt like he had been through this many times already. It never got easier. Everytime, he felt, only left him more broken.

When he walked out of the room with the rest of his family, everybody started asking him questions. Allan couldn't register anything from anyone. He just sat down, and shut down.

Over the next hour, no one could relax. Everyone was hurting everywhere in body, mind, and heart. No one could say a word. It took more strength than anyone had to hold themselves together.

Finally the doctor walked in and huffed exhausted.

"He's stable for now. But it's no fun. Adam's lost so much healthy blood I wanted him back on treatment. Right now, he's in children's ICU."

Allan stayed right next to his son. He didn't go home for three days. Everytime Chris visited, Allan was sleepless, and could hardly speak.

"We'll have to teach Anothy how to yell for help if something like this happens again," Chris said. "We should teach him how to call 911."

Allan could barely acknowledge anything Chris asked or said.

Meanwhile at home, Anthony had done nothing but cry for his brother. He kept begging the family, "Before he goes to see Mommy and Amanda, I really need to see him again!"

***

The morning of the fourth day, before Allan was barely awake. Any moment he was waiting for the alarm to sound, and Adam would be gone...

"Daddy?"

Allan jumped out of his seat.

Adam's eyes were open and he was looking at his father. "Why am I here again?"

Allan walked over to Adam and smiled full. "Oh, hi son," he spoke lovingly, making the moment special. "We had to bring you here because you...you almost died at Mark's Big Pizza Barn." He spoke through his sobs.

"Well, Dad my head was hurting so bad," Adam said. "I told Anthony to get Chris, and now I wake up here at this stupid place again."

Chris arrived shortly with Anthony. When Anothy saw Adam was awake he ran over to his side, and the boys were just talking to each other, as always in what seemed like their own language that they could understand.

Later when the sun had come up, they moved Adam to his own room.

Amy was still in jail and trying to get Alex to come bail her out.

Alex told Amy she was staying there. She needed to understand that her actions had consequences.

"I don't care anymore," he said. "I can't care anymore."

"Alex, please bail me out!" she pleaded. "Let me come back home. I promise I will never do anything like this again, Please Alex!"

"Even if I do, how do I know you won't leave me again?"

"We can have it wrtten out by a lawyer!" Amy said. "You can add whatever else you want to put there, please Alex come and bail me out of jail!"

Alex was only exhausted. At this point, in his life he was wondering what love was anymore.

"Let me just...think about this before I say anything, all right? Give me one hour and call me back. I'll give you your answer then."

Alex called his father and asked him for his advice.

"Are you sure you want to do that?" Allan asked him. "You've had enough craziness in your life."

"I know, but...it feels hard. When she gets like this, it hurts and I do want to let her back in."

"Even if you have a lawyer holding her to it, love doesn't just...work that way," Allan said. "It takes more than a legal contract holding someone to their word to make them not only love you but stay loyal to you. They have to want you, respect you, and sacrifice for you."

Alex groaned, feeling he was being pulled in all directions.

When Amy called Alex again in an hour, he in the middle of talking tot he bail bondsman.

"It will be $2,000, If you want to bail her out," he said. "Remember, if she goes to court, you will get your money back."

"All right," Alex said. "And how long will I have to wait before I can bail her out?"

"Not very long. All I need for you to do is sign a form, submit your ID. It's no longer than a 2 hour process."

***

Hours later, Alex was waiting to see Amy, after having paid her bail.

She came walking out to meet him.

"What the hell took you so long to get me out of this fucking place!" she asked.

Already Alex was feeling sorry about what he'd done, but he had to follow through now.

"Okay Amy," he said. "Tomorrow we are going to a lawyer's office and have those papers drawn up. I am going to write out my terms and you can read it."

***

At midnight that night, Adam flatlined again.

The hospital called code blue.

Allan was kicked out of the room. Not one word was said this time.

About one hour later the doctor came in, with two words.

"I'm sorry."

Back home, Anthony woke up yelling and screaming for somebody to take him to Adam. No one understood what had gotten into him.

***

Allan didn't wan't to go home. He went to his private work office that night.

He cried in a corner, in a fetal position there.

"God," he sobbed. "You have two of my children and Anna. What did I do? What did I do that was so bad that you have taken my wife and two of my children?"

Allan cried all night long. He didn't know how he was going to tell Anthony that his twin was dead. Every time he would think about how to say it, he could only foresee how awful Anthony was going to take the news. He didn't even want to tell the others.

Before sunrise, Allan left his office and went home. When he came in through the door, Anthony was right there crying so hard. All Allan could do was pick up his son and comfort him. They went to Allan's bedroom and sat on the bed.

Anthony was still in his father's arms. Anthony looked up at his father and sobbed, "Did God take my brother too, Daddy?"

Allan could only cry about and finally answered "Yes. Adam is now with God."

Anthony, that little boy, looked at his father, clenching his jaw. He got off the bed and turns to his Father and said, "I don't ever want to hear that word, 'God' again! I really, really hate God! I will never talk to him again!"

Anthony ran into his bedroom and slammed the door very

hard and was crying so loud and just throwing stuff around in his room.

Chris and Andrew tried to open the door, but Anthony had put his chair in front of the door so nobody could open it. Anthony stayed in his room all day and night.

That was when Alex came home with Amy.

Amy knocked on Anthony's door several times.

"Anthony," she said. "It's your aunt Amy. Can I please come in so I can talk to you? Please, Anthony?"

At last, Anthony opened his door, not only for Amy, but for Allan and Chris, who were standing there too. He was looking at the ground, face red, tears dried on his cheeks.

"Can I go see Adam?" he asked. "One last time?"

"All right," Allan said. "Get dressed and I'll take you with Alex and Amy."

An hour later, Amy and Alex took Anthony to see his brother.

Allan left them at the Hospital and drove off. He wasn't ready yet.

***

The two nurses stood outside the door, while Alex and Amy stayed in the waiting room.

Anthony walked into Adam's room to see his brother one last time. Adam's color had left his face and he was still.

Little Anthony tried to talk to his brother in their special babbling again. But as he spoke, he realized he didn't know how anymore.

At last, all he could do was break down besides Adam, defeated, hurt, and in awful pain. He had scarcely done so, when Adam sat up, shouting, "Anthony! Anthony!"

The nurses froze in the doorway, shocked!

Anthony looked up and saw Adam's color had come back. His eyes were opened wide and and he was smiling brightly.

One of the nurses came in. "Now, you two young men don't go anywhere! The doctor's on his way."

***

"Allan!" Amy called Allan's cell phone. "Get back to the Hospital now! You have to get back to the hospital right now!"

Allan turned around and drove straight back to the hospital, nearly flooring the pedal. He parked. He ran in, he hurried straight for Adam's room. Hospital staff had surrounded Adam's bed, Alex and Amy were beaming.

Finally the staff parted and urgently beckoned Allan to come in.

Adam was siting up in bed happily next to Anothy. The twins were just playing with each other.

"Adam?!" Allan gasped. "You're not dead!"

Allan came forward and reached for for Adam. Adam reached back. Allan felt Adam's hands and arms gripping him with strength. He hugged around his son, feeling a beating heart and breathing! He couldn't believe it. He didn't understand, but he didn't care.

The doctor walked in with papers in his hands. The nurses kept asked what the latest tests revealed.

"There's no cancer in his body," the doctor said.

Everyone looked shocked.

"I know!" Adam said. "I had to go see Mommy! She said the cancer would be taken from me!"

"What?" Allan asked, first.

Adam told the story for everyone in the room.

"I went to sleep and Mommy came to me! We hugged eachother and she kissed my head."

Adam placed his palm on his forehead.

Allan blinked, and could only breath the name, "Anna."

"She told me all my cancer was going away. And it did!" Adam said. "Now I have no more cancer!"

Alex walked forward, looking stunned.

"You saw Mom?" he asked.

***

Allan was able to bring home, when they walked in, seeing Adam with them, they were shocked.

"Is this some kind of joke?!" Andrew asked. Those were the words that came out, the only world he could think of.

Adam was greeting with many hugs, holding, and happy tears, words of gladness and love.

When asked what had happened, everyone sat down in the living room and Adam again gave his account to them all.

"She said she loved everyone of us!" Adam said. "She said she was watching all of us, even at Mark's Big Pizza Barn. She said she loved everyone and said everyone by name!"

Adam proceeded to name everyone in his family, and he

pointed to each one. All his brothers his brothers and sisters, and his father. He even said Amanda's name.

***

A year passed.

Amy was living with Alex again. They even had another baby girl–whom they named Ashley.

Early in June, the family got a call from Allison at bootcamp. Amber picked up.

"I need to talk to Daddy, it's very important," Allison said. "Can you please get him on the phone?"

Allan was already walking up. Amber gave the phone to him.

"I'm here, Allison," he said. "What did you need?"

"I need for you to come pick me up," Allisons said. "I just got kicked out of bootcamp school."

"And why is that?" Allan asked. "What did you do this time?"

"Dad I didn't do anything this time!"

"Well I'm calling your teacher and she what she says."

Allison's instructor gave a very different account from.

When Allan got off the phone and heard everything her instructor had told him, he called Allison back and told her, "You better have everything ready and packed by the time I get there. I'll see you about one hour."

***

Allan drove fast. He was very upset at Allison. Several times his cellphone rang, but he didn't want to answer it.

177

When he arrived at Bootcamp, Allison was not packed at all. She was sitting outside, crying and not doing anything.

Allan got out of the car and shouted, "Allison, you should ben have been packed by now! You better get off your ass and go pack your stuff."

Allison's instructor came out and told him, "Sir, we tried to contact you. We are going to give her one more chance here at our school. She is performing well, and has all A's right now. Her behavior does need work, so we are putting her in one-hour after school study, Monday and Wednesday. For twenty days. But the next time she gets into any kind of a fight, she *will* be kicked out of school."

*** 

Andy was only seven years old, and would be going the third grade that summer later that August. In the meantime, Andy, Andrew, and Chris, were the happiest when all three of them were together. They got along so harmoniously, even if they were different ages.

One Friday, Chris, Andy, and Andrew all wanted to go to the drive-in movies and get something to eat afterward. Allan let Andy go with the two older men.

"Andy you will need your pillow and a blanket, because it will be late when we get home, you might fall asleep."

The three men left that night, they left at sundown.

Alyssa had a date that evening, and Amber just wanted to stay home like always. Allan and twins we are going to Mark's Big Pizza Barn again to celebrate a second time. They asked Amber if

178

she wanted to go, but she told them no. She wished them a fun time.

Alex and Amy called Amber and asked her to babysit their two kids at their home. Amber agreed as long as she was paid.

"We can pay you, yes. And on your way back, can you carry something big to your house?"

"I don't know. Depending on how big it is," Amber replied. "Why don't you just use your car and drop them off for me along with it."

"All right, we'll do that. We're on our way."

***

Once Alex and Amy arrived with their girls, they asked where everyone was.

"Andy to the drive-in movies with Chris and Andrew. Alyssa is out on a date, and dad with the twins and Allison went to Mark's Big Pizza Barn."

"And you're just stay home? Why don't you want to go out anymore?"

"I do wanna go out but I'm just not ready to put myself out there yet, you know?" Amber said. "I still love school and I want to be my best. I don't want to date or anything like that right now."

"All right," Alex said. "You know how to feed Ashley and Alice right?"

"Yes, Alex I know all that shit," Amber said with a smile.

"Good. See you around midnight, or no later than 1:00 in the morning. Thank you for this."

The twin boys came home with Allan came home at 9

o'clock that evening. Alice was getting into everything she could get her hands on. Ashley kept babbling away to Amber, whilst Amber held her and talked back pleasantly.

When Allan walked in the house, Alice let out a big scream.

"Alice where are you?" Amber asked.

Alice shouted, "I'm in your room!" and started to cry loudly.

Amber got up to her room and saw that Alice had pulled the table over on top of herself. She couldn't get out of it. She wasn't hurt, so Amber laid the baby down and helped Alice up. They went downstairs and Allan played a little game by hiding and saying, "I see you. I can see you, Alice."

He jumped out from behind the couch saying, "Boo!"

When Alice saw her grandpa, she went running to him happily. He picked her up.

"What's Grandpa's little gal doing at his house?" Allan laughed.

"Mommy and daddy go bye-bye, so I'm with Aunt Amber."

The twins ran up straight to their room, and Alice wanted to follow them.

Amber said, "Dad I'm going to go to Alex's house so I can put Alice and Ashley down for the night."

"Sounds good," said Allan. "I'll give you a ride back there."

\*\*\*

Amber got the two girls into their pajamas at Alex's house after a warm bath. Alice thought is was so funny, now, that tonight Amber's little table felt on her today and kept talking about it. Amber fed them both before bed. Alice went right to sleep, however, Ashley was not going to bed for anything.

Amber went between sitting in a rocking chair with Ashley and gave her a bottle, to walking around with her in her arms. When Alex and Amy came in from their date night, they asked how much do we owe you?"

"Sixty-five dollars for the two of them," Amber said.

"Sure," said Alex. "And hey, on Friday nights, would you be able to babysit for the two girls again? We'll pay you the same again, and if we stay out *real* late we will pay you extra money."

"Yeah, I guess I can try that for a while, at least," Amber said. "And hey, Alex, do you think on Monday you will help me get a savings account? I want to put my money in the bank, when you pay me."

"Wow, Amber, you really are going to show all the others that you're doing your best. You set a great example for others."

\*\*\*

That autumn, the family felt they were starting to get everything together. Everyone knew their routines, life was looking up for everyone.

On the last day of the semester, Andy walked right into the house and went right up to his room and closed his door. He wouldn't talk to anyone, not even Chris and Andrew.

When he heard his father pull up into the driveway, he ran out of his room and into his father's office.

Allan met him there. "Hey Andy," he said. "Chris and

Andrew told me you haven't talked to anyone today. Can I help you with something?"

Andy nodded. "I wanted you to be the first to know."

He handed Allan his report card, in addition to a letter form his teacher.

Allan opened Andy's report card, and read the letter. Allan smiled and hugged his son.

"I am so proud of you!" he said.

# Chapter 10

Andy was a very smart child. He'd skipped two grades, but now teachers were suggesting advancing him two more to place an eight-year-old in fifth grade. Allan resisted, wanting Andy to stay at his age level for emotional comfort. Allan argued for pushing ahead, but Andy's resolve was firm.

"Dad," Andy said, "I just don't want to be the youngest kid in fifth grade. I don't like the idea of being bullied because everyone thinks I'm too smart. I'd rather not stand out."

Allan knelt beside him. "We'll figure it out, son. It's okay."

***

Later, Andy left Allan's office after overhearing the conversation about his grades. Kristen found him frowning and asked, "Why were you so upset?"
Andy sighed. "I got a letter from my teacher for Dad—she wants me moved up two more grades. I don't want that. The kids will bully me because I'm the youngest in fifth grade. They'll torment me until I crack."

Chris paused.

"What about when you hit sixth or seventh grade? You'll still jump straight to tenth by senior year. What do you want to do then?"

Andy's voice steadied. "If anything, I want to be the best lawyer in this world. To help people fight for what they believe in —not just adults, but kids too... especially those whose parents don't want them."

"Why a lawyer?"

"To give them someone who'll stand up for them when no one else will," he said softly.

"Andy, do you remember when Andrew first came here? The way you treated him?" Chris asked.

"Yes sir."

"But you never disrespected him. That's why I knew you'd work great with the kids."

Andrew stepped into the doorway at that moment and Chris saw him. He then looked over at Allan saying, "That reminds me. Sir, if I could have a word with you?"

Andy left the office and left Allan alone with Chris and Andre.

"Is there something wrong?" Allan asked.

Chris steepled his fingers and said flatly, "No sir. Andrew and I've been talking. We want to do something really good."

"Come on, Chris—what's this?" Allan asked.

Chris gestured at Andrew. "Hit it."

Andrew leaned forward, saying, "Why not open a home? For kids whose parents don't want them. Like a brother-sister club! A place to hang out by day, hang out at night... somewhere safe." He paused. "Does that make sense?"

"You want my help with this?" Allan asked, interest radiating from his face.

"We're thinking names," said Chris. "Amanda's Brother & Sister Club? Or, 'A Million Brothers & Sisters'? Maybe just, 'Amanda's Clubhouse for All Children.'"

"No no—listen!" Andrew barked, grinning. "Amanda's Club For All Kiddos! Underneath that, we'll write... something about staying in school, right?"

"You came up with all this!" Chris said. "It's natural to you. But how do we house them? Keep 'em safe at night?"

Allan rubbed his temples, but was smiling. "Well, let me sleep on it—two days. I'll figure out the details if I can."

Both men thanks Allan and left him to work.

Allan wasn't able to to get too far before Allison called.

"This better be good," he muttered, answering. "Hello?"

"Dad?" Allison asked. "Can I come home for the weekend? There's something I want to talk to you guys about."

Allan felt his gut clench. "All right. I hope everything is ok."

After hanging up, Allan went down stairs with wallet, phone, and keys.

"Chris, I'm picking up Allison, she's coming to stay for the weekend. Can you get pizza for dinner?"

"Well yeah—but all of us were going to get burgers."

\*\*\*

Allan drove Allison home down the highway. She was quiet

185

for half the way home before she spoke up.

"Daddy... can I ask you a question?

Allan kept his eyes on the highway. "Sure, what's up?"

Her voice cracked. "Why did Mom leave all of us? Why just take the twins? Did I do something wrong? Did she hate me?"

He pulled into a rest area, already fighting tears. "No, sweetheart—it wasn't your fault. It was my fault... both times. Allison, what happened with your mom and me is between us. It has nothing to do with you kids." He paused. "But if you want the truth..."

Allison nodded, and Allan pulled into the nearest rest stop first.

"Your mother started seeing Tom before we were married," Allan said, his voice raw. "She had Alyssa and Amber with *him*... then you came. By the time you turned two, I found out everything. I made her leave—but Amanda wanted to stay with her mom. She ran away, hid in your mother's car..."

Allison stared at him. "Mom was married to him? Why she'd break up with him?"

"Because of what he did to you girls," Allan swallowed hard. "Tom raped Alyssa and Amanda... Your real father is the one who hurt them. I adopted you three after your real father landed in jail for it. He's still there, last I heard."

Allison's hands shook, her eyes gazing at Allan for who he was—her adoptive father.

After a thick silence, Allison proceeded, "And Mom didn't know?"

"She heard, but she didn't believe it," Allan said. "Until she walked in on it herself."

Allison trembled visibly. "Even if she only heard, why didn't she suspect that maybe...just maybe..."

Allan closed his eyes, "She loved Tom," he said. "Even after what he did. That got between everything." Allan looked up and continued, "Well," he said. "Maybe *that* wasn't love. But attachment. Love isn't the same as that. But Allison," Allan said, locking his eyes with her own. "Anna...loves you," he said. "She always has. And so do I."

***

Everyone was happy to see Allison again. Andy ran and jumped into Allison's arms and hugged her then said.

"Allison, you didn't get into any kind of trouble, did you?"

"No Andy, I just wanted to come home because I miss my family and you so much!" Allison said. "Andy can I sleep in your room tonight please brother?"

"Yes!" Andy replied.

We went and got his room ready for Allison's stay.

When Amber heard her sister's voice she ran downstairs and cried for joy.

Alyssa still had a problem with Allison, having seen how she spoke to Chris.

Andy mentioned to Allison about his trip with Chris and Andrew. They were taking him out again tonight.

"Daddy, you let Andy go to the drive with these two men?" Allison asked.

"Yes," Allan said. "They are always together these days and I am very happy that Andy has these two friends because they love that boy so much."

Allison said to Chris, "All right," she said. "Please take care of my little brother tonight."

Chis look at Allison and didn't say a word to her, walking right past her. But there was a knowing gleam in his eye. Allison was acting too good. Since she had come home, she'd been talking overly sweet, all smiles, and showing puppy-dog eyes.

Allan only said, "Have fun you three kids."

When they had left through the front door, Alisson could only asked, "What is wrong with Chris? He didn't say one word to me."

***

That night when Alyssa had come home from her date, was there to greet her.

"Hi sister! How are you?"

Alyssa walked right by her. "When you respect everybody in your home then I'll talk to you. But I'm fine. Thank you."

Alyssa went straight to her room.

Allison followed her up and knocked on her sister's door.

"Come in," said Alyssa.

Alisson walked in. "Did I disrespect you, sister? I'm so so sorry I didn't mean to."

Alyssa said, "No you didn't, but I remember how bad you did with Chris." Alyssa did a double take with Alisson and huffed. "What is this all about? You're hiding something. Or you want

188

something? What is it?"

Alisson's mask came off and she shut the door behind her, speaking quietly.

"I wanted to come home this weekend because I need to talk to you and Amber about something."

"What is that?"

"Do you know your our mom was married to Allan?"

Alyssa flinched when Alisson called Allan by name.

"Then Mom met our father. Our real father, Tom." Alisson said. "She married him as well? She was married to two men at the same time. I was 4 years old when Allan adopted all three of us girls."

"I know all of this Allison," Alyssa said. "And Tom went to jail for raping our two sisters, and as far I'm concerned he can rot there."

Alisson glared at Alyssa. "Tom's not in jail," she said. "He found me there at boot camp. He wants all of us to move back to Vegas. To our home we've always had."

Alyssa froze.

Alisson grimaced and began bark bitterly. Spitefully. "And I'm going! I never want to see Allan again!"

"'Allan,'" Alyssa said, "is our *father*!"

"Not mine! I just need to talk to Amber and see if she is going to go back too! I'm sick of this life here!"

"You are crazy!" Alyssa said.

"This whole house is crazy! Why should I stay here and I

189

get sent off to boot camp without a choice in it all?! Because of Allan and Chris! So I'm going back home!"

At that moment, Amber walked in.

"Is something going on in here?"

*** 

Moments later, Amber came running out of her room and right to her Allan's arms, crying. "Daddy!" she said. She was outright quaking traumatically.

"Alisson is saying you adopted all three of us girls, and that are real father has asked us girls to...to come move back to vegas!"

"What" Allan asked.

"She says Tom found her at Bootcamp! Allison wants to go back with him! She was asking me if I was coming with her!" Amber broke down.

Allan held Amber tightly and comfortingly. "You're safe. I promise," he told her, than stood up and shouted, "Allison! Get your ass up here now! Get into my office!"

Allison went begrudgingly marched into Allan's office, while Allan phoned Chris,

"Chris," he said. "You need bring Andy home, immediately."

Allan went into his office where Allison was glaring defiantly.

"Sit in the fucking chair! Now!" Allan commanded. *"This* why you came home this weekend?"

"Yes sir," Allison groaned, standing. "You're not my dad, and you can't you keep me here If I'm not your daughter."

"Allison, I am your dad, because Tom gave you girls to me when he raped both your sisters! So no! You may not go anywhere around him at all! Now go to your room and stay there until I come and get you!"

***

Chris came home with Andrew and Andy. Allan brought Chris and Andrew into his office and told Andy, "Can you go out for this one please, son?"

Andy left and Allan shut the door, talking to both Chris and Andrew.

"All right," he said. "Remember Tom? That guy who raped both girls?"

"Yes," Chris said.

"He's found Allison at school. He wants her to move back to Vegas with him. Alisson even tried to convice Amber to go with her."

Chris frowned, and nodded stoically. "So what do you want to do?"

***

Alex left his Father, along with Chris and Andrew that night. He told, Amy, "Stay with our kids until we get back. And do not let Allison out of her room."

None one else knew what was going on.

Alisson did not leave her room. Amber took her up some snacks periodically, but she didn't try to talk to her.

***

Allan, Chris, Andrew, and Alex were on the road that same

night.

"Dad," Alex said. "Once Alisson turns eighteen, she might just leave and go to him on her own, and then there really won't be anything we can do, even legally."

Allan's grip on the wheel tightened. The road lead deeper into desert mountains. The light of Vegas beaming over the next incline.

"Then we make sure he doesn't want her back by then."

***

Allan knocked hard on Tom's door.

When it opened, Allan's hand curled into a fist.

"You're the son of a bitch who married my wife while she was still mine," he was snarling like a wolf ready to tear out guts. "And I've legally adopted all three girls. You have zero rights to them—not after what you did."

Tom's smirk didn't waver. "I'll bet you can't keep me away forever, Allan."

Chris stepped forward, jaw tight. "Try crossing paths with us again, and we'll bury you six feet deep. Understand?"

Alex nodded grimly behind him, a silent echo of threat.

Tom's defiance faltered. "Why can't I see my daughters? They're my girls."

"You raped them!" Allan barked loud and clear for the street. "They don't belong to you—and they never will."

Chris joined in, "If you're seen near our home or the girls' school, the cops get called—and it'll be your funeral!"

Tom's voice softened, playing the wounded father. "I just

want one visit. Please, Allan. They're my daughter's too. Can you ask the girls if they want to see me? If they say, 'No,' I'll leave them alone."

"You are not listening!" Allan roared. "Listen to me! You stay away from my daughters! You hurt them! You lost them! I don't care if they do want to see you again. If I find you with them, I will send you straight to hell!"

Tom closed the door. "Get off of my property!" he shouted. "Or I call the cops!"

Allan grimaced and turned around, headed back for the car with the other men.

***

When they arrived home it was sunrise.

Allison didn't want to talk to him.

Allan grabbed three cups of coffee and took them to his office to work. He kept pondering what to do—how to protect his children from that man—especially Allison.

He knew Alex was right. When Allison turned eighteen, there was no stopping her from choosing to live with Tom. Allan didn't care how old Allison turned—she was still his daughter. The thought of her being in the same space as Tom, breathing the same air, made him viscerally sick.

Allan's phone rang—a number from Las Vegas.

He answered.

"Allan?" Tom's voice asked. He was sobbing. "Please, I know what I did was wrong. I can't stomach that I did anything to them. I just want one more day. At least think about it. After one more day, I'll never speak to them again. I promise. You have my word! Talk to Anna. All of us can talk about this!"

"You know their mother passed away?" Allan said.

Tom sobbed and sneered audibly. "You mean my wife, long before you two got married? Yes, you stole my wife! How would you know if the girls are even yours?"

"They *are* mine," Allan said. "They are *not* yours. And if you want to speak to me again about this, it will have to be from your lawyer. Even then, as a lawyer myself, I would say your chances of seeing those kids are shit!"

"Just one day!" Tom cried bitterly. "Just one day!"

"You live with the consequences of your crimes," Allan said. "You sorry son of a bitch. You should be grateful enough you're not behind bars. Take whatever you got left and make the most of your life if you're serious–that's as much compassion as I can offer to you. But one thing's for certain: you don't ever come to my kids, or I'll put you in hell."

Allan hung up.

Exhausted, frightful, and weary, he couldn't work.

He fell asleep in his chair.

He didn't even come down to dinner that evening.

Allan felt he was becoming primal. He was broken from everything his family had been through. Now Tom was back in the picture, and he was ready to fight savage for love of his daughters if he had to.

***

Allan leaned against the passenger door of the van. His

194

shirt clung to him—stiff with yesterday's coffee stains and the sweat of restless hours. He hadn't showered, hadn't eaten. The ache behind his eyes mirrored the weight of Allison's fury.

"Why does Chris have to take me back to schoo?" Allison snapped, arms crossed against. "You're not my dad—you don't get to—"

Chris stepped forward, blocking Allan's view of her face. "Your dad asked me," he said assertively. "He can't do this right now."

Allison turned her back on both of them, stalking toward the van, her boots crunching gravel. The door slammed behind her.

Allan saw Allisons defiance. He let in a breath, but his chest tightened. His throat burned with words he wanted to tell his daughter—words of love and compassion. He kept telling himself now was not the time. He needed to hold onto control for now.

Allan handed Chris the keys. "Just...get her there in one piece," he said.

Chris nodded once, already moving toward the driver's side. The engine roared to life again.

Allan stood rooted as the van peeled away, stirring dust into the still air. He didn't move until its taillights vanished over the hill.

# Chapter 11

"Allison," Chris said, "On this road trip, you and I are going to get to know each other better by asking each other questions. Ok?"

Allison was quiet as Chris drove her to Boot Camp.

"May I go first?" she asked.

"Yes, that would be nice of you. First the rules: you have to tell the truth, no matter what. No asking about our sex lives."

"All right. How long have you been doing your job working with children?"

"I found out one night that I could never have kids of my own. So I started working with kids for others. My turn. Allison, what did I do to you to make you treat me like shit?"

"You were always in my business," Allison groaned. "You're not my father, he ought to tell me what to do. Plus you always went right after me no matter what like everything was my fault. My turn next. do you really love your job with my family?"

"Yes, I really love my work with all of you. Truth be told Allison, I liked working with you best, until you started talking to me the way you do. My next question: do you really like being at boot camp?"

"Yes and no," Allison replied. "Yes, because like going there because my grades are so good. No. because I miss my whole family. And I really miss you the most. Chris, would you forgive me for the way I talk to you?"

"Of course I would, kiddo," Chris said. "I do forgive you. But I expect you to do better from here on out. My next question: do you want to come back home?"

Allison looked out the window. "Yes and no," she said. "No, because I love how my school runs itself and my teachers and everything. Yes, because, again, I miss my whole family. I don't want my grades to go bad, though."

***

On the way home, they stopped at Chris's favorite place to eat–a burger diner.

"Wow, I have never been here yet," Allison said, stepping inside the checker-pattern tiled floor. "Do they have real good food?"

"The best ever," answered Chris.

Allison was floored at how everything was so big as well a decadent, from the milkshakes in the metal jugs to the seasoned fries. She wanted to take pictures of everything that she could.

Her burger had blue cheese dressing–after the first bite she promised she would tell her father about this place.

***

When they they back on the road, Chris continued, "Allison, when you say I was 'all in your business,' I really want you to know I was just showing you how much I really love you. Sometimes, loving someone means making sure they are safe, and sometimes it means discipline is needed too. Love doesn't mean we stay idle and live and let live all the time."

Allison didn't say anything. She just looked outside the window. She listened to Chris, but didn't feel like taking everything in.

"Among your sisters, you were once one of the most enjoyable to work with. Like, among the boys, Andy is my number one buddy. He and Andrew make me laugh so hard because of the shit they pull on each other. The jokes they play and the play fighting they love doing."

Chris must have seen Allison wasn't engaged, so he changed the subject.

"What is boot camp school like?"

"It's nothing like the school anyone else goes to," Allison answered. "We get up at six, and at seven we've had breakfast. Rooms need to be cleaned half an hour later. Then the actual school happens. We all wear the same thing every day. Every day. At noon, we have lunch, and dinner is at six, and all homework need be done before dinner. Then we go to the store, get to call home, or just hang out and watch TV or read. All lights are out by ten at night."

"You have the schedule down I see." Chris said.

He pulled up into the parking lot. Allison sighed and gathered her belongings.

"Good luck, Allison," Chris said.

"Thanks," Allison replied, nonchalantly, walking into the building.

At least some acknowledgement was better than none, thought Chris.

***

When Chris got home, he had dinner boxes for all the family–he had picked up burgers from the same diner he had showed to Allison.

Alex and Amy, as well as both of their girls were there as well.

Allan looked at Chris, having cleaned up. "Thank you for doing this," he said. "You didn't have to go the extra mile with dinner."

Everyone thanked Chris and mentioned how delicious the food was. Allan even mentioned how he loved the blue cheese dressing on his hamburger.

After dinner, Allan looked called Alyssa and Amber and asked them gently, "Can I see you both in my office please?"

Both Amber and Alyssa walking upstairs to Allan's office. Allan stayed behind and waited until they were out of earshot and told Chris to wait nearby.

"I'm going to sit Alyssa and Amber down and tell them what is going on, with Allison. Tom too," he said. So stand by, because I don't know how this will play out. I hope it all goes right."

Chris nodded devotedly. "I'll be right here, sir. For them both."

Allan walked upstairs and met with his two daughters.

"What's going on, Daddy?"

Allan sat them both down and told them. "Wait until I finish talking," he told them. "Get comfortable, because we need to revisist some tragic memories. I'll be here with you."

Allysa and Amber got comfortable as they could. Allan felt heavy inside as he braced to tell them.

"So, you know I adopted you three girls years ago–both of you and Allison. Allison was only three years old when I adopted my girls. Your mother and I were married for five years and then she had you, Alyssa. Then we were still married and she married another man. That was Tom, your real father.

"I went to New York where your mother said she worked sometimes, and that is when I had found out that she had two husbands. I found out she was living in Vegas with your father. Your mother tried to hide it by telling me that Tom man was her best friend's husband and that your, Amber, were his kid. I really didn't want to hear it, then, so I made her leave.

"One night Amanda...your sister...was raped by your real dad. Your mother didn't believe her for a long time, until she came home and walked in on it happening. That's when we put him in jail. That brings us to today."

Allan braced himself. "Tom is now out of jail. Tom is saying he really wants to see you girls, so he found Allison at boot camp school."

Alyssa and Amber quaked visibly.

"I went to go talk to Tom that night. I was there with Chris and Andrew, and your brother Alex. We warned him not to come near any of you. Personally. He's now saying he wants to see you girls, just once, for even just one day and then he say's he'll leave you alone. But I don't want any of you going near him at all."

Amber stood up, visibly rattling, nodding. "You are my dad. *You* are!" She said. "Not this Tom guy. I don't want to see him ever!"

"Same here," Amber sobbed. "He raped me, why would I ever want that good for nothing son of a bitch again in my life?!"

"I know, I know," Allan said, holding them both with care. "I needed to let you know so you can be watchful of him."

Alyssa continued to sob. "I don't want to see him at all. Ever again."

"I know, sweethearts," Allan said. "Look out for each other. I'll look out for you both too. I promise."

After comforting them, Allan told them both, "I have some phone calls to make. I'll check up on you again soon."

***

Later in the week Allan tried calling Allison. It had been a while and he wanted to check up on her.

She didn't answer the phone. Allan called the school.

"Hello," Allan said. "May I speak to Allison? It's her father, Allan."

"Allan?" the receptionist answered. "Allison isn't here. She said you were picking her up for dinner."

Allan's heart dropped cold.

"When did Allison leave?" he asked.

"Allison hasn't been here for four days."

Allan hung up, sweating cold, blood boiling.

"That's my cue to really hurt some son of a bitch."

***

Allan drove up to Tom's house, directly in his driveway, finding a strange elderly man seated on the porch. The elder rose up asking in alarm, "Can I help you sir?"

Allan got out of the car and asked, "Where is Tom?"

"Tom?"

"The man who owns this house," Allan said.

The elder took a minute to think. "Tom? I haven't seen him for four days now."

"Do you know where he could have gone?" Allan asked. "It's an emergency."

"Said he'd be up in another house, up in the hills somewhere. I know which one, though."

***

Another hour's drive and Allan found the house. He stopped the car at the other end of the road and walked up.

Tom opened the door, presumably to run an errand, but when he saw Allan walking up, Allan kicked the door back, roaring, "Where is my daughter!?!"

Tom crumpled to the floor, trembling. "I don't know what are you talking about!"

*"Bullshit!"* Allan bared his teeth, flipping over Tom's Television followed by the small dining table.

"Honest sir-!" Tom quaked, terrified. "There's no one here but me!"

Allan heard something... from further down the halls, he

202

went to the door, hearing Tom huffing and panting in terror. A girls gagged voice was trying to sob through the door. Allan's hand went for the knob—it was fastened with a heavy combination lock.

Allan grabbed Tom by the arms as he was scrambling to get out of the house and run to his car.

"Unlock this fucking door!" Allan roared, forcing Tom back inside.

"No!" Tom yelled frightfully.

*"Do it now!"* Allan roared. *"You sorry son of a bitch!"*

"I won't!" Tom screamed.

Allan threw Tom against a cabinet ont he wall, glass breaking in the wake of his tumble. Allan turned and bull rushed the wooden door—out of his sheer strength, the heavy combination lock didn't matter—the old hinges busted.

Allison was naked and tied up to the bed.

Allan's heart was broken and his tears poured like waterfalls. "The cops are on the way!" he sobbed. "Hold on, baby! I can't touch anything here until the cops show up."

No sooner, sirens could be heard on the air.

# Chapter 12

Allison was taken up to a hospital and evaluated.

Afterward, Allan took her home by plane.

Chris was there at the airport to pick them up. When Allison saw Chris, she ran over to him and put her in his arms, crying for comfort. She couldn't speak any words through her sobbing, but none were needed. Chris knew Allison understood at last she was home. He held her safe. He was so sorry he hadn't done more, but grateful she was safe now.

Counseling was offered to her throughout the next months.

***

Alyssa started college in the fall, two years later, Amber did as well. They both went to the same college–one in New York.

Andy continued into high school, and during those years, the twin boys started junior high school. Chris was still with them.

By then Alex had five kids total: Alice, Ashley, Autumn, Ava, and Arnold.

In the years that followed, Alyssa married and was going to have her first baby: a boy whom she named Donnie.

Allan passed away later before Donnie was born.

He was missed greatly by everyone in the family, Chris and Andrew included.

Shortly before Alyssa's baby boy was due, Amy announced she was going to have her sixth baby.

Andrew also was married during that time.

Amber married as well and announced she was having her first baby during an Easter Sunday dinner at the house with the family.

Allison spent many busy nights having fun at parties when she went into college. Once a month, Allison would show up for a Sunday dinner.

After graduating from high school, Andy went to Rome. He ended up studied in Germany for the next year.

The twin boys started high school later on. As they were both contemplating their future, they both wanted to go to different colleges.

However, during the summer, Adam got very sick again.

Chris took him to the doctor, and they discovered his cancer had back. It was terminal. Adam told Chris not to tell anybody in the family until he was ready to make the announcement himself.

He didn't want anyone to mourn him.

Anothy started the eleven grade alone that year—Adam staying home, getting sicker by the day.

Allison started drinking and doing drugs, that summer. No one knew until Chris got a call from his phone from her from jail.

She had been arrested for driving under the influence. Police had also uncovered she was selling drugs.

"You need to get your ass home and stay there," Chris told her–Allision being too inebriated to think coherently.

When Chris told Andy and the boys, they were extremely disappointed in her.

The college did not allow Allison to return thereafter.

Andrew's marriage was short-lived, unfortunately. His wife divorced him and started dating a younger man.

Andy surprised his family by coming home for Christmas. He also brought his girlfriend from Germany. They had been dating for the last four month. He loved her very much.

Anna Lee was her name. She was the one who wanted Andy to surprise them with the news–so they would have something special for Christmas.

Anthony told Andy that he wanted to go to Germany next summer to see what it looked like.

The night before going back to Germany, Andy told Chris privately that he didn't know if he would see Adam again.

"But I love my brother," Andy said. "I hugged him long, this morning, and just told him how much I love him."

***

In, February Chris called Andy to let me know that Adam had died in Anthony's arms.

Andy told him, "Thank you for letting me know. When will you put him to rest?"

"Not until next week."

"All right," Andy said. "I'll be there."

"Is Anna Lee coming with you?" Chris asked.

"Hell no," Andy said. "We broke up. But I suppose better now than later."

Chris nodded. "That's what careful dating is for: finding out."

***

The day after Adam had passed, Allison had to be in court. Unfortunately, no one could find her. The judge issued a warrant.

She was found in Vegas after an extensive search.

The judge went easy on her at first.

However, Allison continued to show up in jail every month like clockwork.

Chris wouldn't let her move back into the house. He also stopped bailing her out.

By summer of that year, the judge threw the book at Allison. She was offered to go to rehabilitation or face 10 years in prison, followed by rehabilitation. Days later, she was bussed to prison. Chris offered to see her off, but she didn't want to see him.

Allison thought prison wouldn't be so bad—no harder than boot camp school. She was gravely wrong.

In May, Andy called home and told Chris that he would not be coming home but one more time. He was going to stay and live there in Germany. He was having the time of his life there, and he visited Rome as well, frequently.

***

Anthony hated going to school without Adam.

Adam had made everything fun for them both. On his first day of 12th, he was a very different person, miserable and cynical. He could only say how much he missed his twin brother.

One evening, Chris came into his room. "Hey Anthrony, do you want to go back to the drive-in movies tonight with Andrew and i?"

"No," Anthony said. "Thank you, Chris."

"Anthony," Chris said, knowingly. "Would you come here please?"

"Yes sir," Anthony relented.

Chris looked at him, seeing Anthony was a shadow of himself with signs of deterioration in many areas of his wellness. "Anthony, are you on drugs?" Chris asked.

"No," Anthony objected with an attitude. "Why, are *you* on drugs?"

\*\*\*

Alex came home to visit the next day. "Chris, I got a letter from Allison. She is doing all right. She is asking us to send her a few things. Say, have you seen Anthony today?"

"Last I saw him, he was in his room last evening."

Alex walked into the bedroom and saw Anthony passed out with a needle in his arm.

Chris called 911 and Anthony was sent to the hospital. The doctor told Alex and Chris that he had overdosed on heroin.

\*\*\*

The many in the family lived in that one house all their lives. Some died. Others went to jail. And with every tragedy, many feared the family would never be the same.

But even if it wasn't, the children among Allan and Anna who endured went on to raise their families in that house. There was still life, light, and joy, and belief in living to be found yet, in spite of everything that had transpired.

There were always children for Chris to watch in that house. Chris never left, but remained like a guardian angel through the generations into his own old age—loving, nurturing, disciplining, and protecting all under that roof. He continued making many memories with the family through the years, and passed down many stories as well as lessons to each new little ones.

No matter how painful any memories, no matter how tragic many stories ended, Allan and Anna's family did not dissolve or see destruction. Rather, it endured whenever they abided in a spirit of love.

The End

# *Courage*

Never give up hope,
And if you can
Find the courage
To love again.

Five minutes, five days
And a lifetime
Forever change
In a single moment.

You should always be looking for love
Only to see
You never know
Who may come along to love you.

Love can be painful
That's why you need to find
The courage to love again

After your heart is broken.

Put hope back
Into your heart
And find the courage
To love again.

-Mary Denise